I SAW THE SAME DREAM, AGAIN!

Guru Prudhvi

Slice of Life Series

Guru Prudhvi

First Edition: 2016

Second Edition: 2019

I saw the same dream, again!

"Dreams say what they mean, but they don't say it in daytime language."

- Gail Godwin

Guru Prudhvi

About the Book

Since childhood, I have been a good listener. This trait of mine qualifies me to act as a friendly counsellor. Playing this role as a friendly counsellor meant that I would come across multiple situations and complexities that one faces in life. Some of my acquaintances share their problems with me, not with the hope that I will solve those but because they feel that I empathise and listen to them. At a selected few such instances, I felt that I was able to connect myself to their situations and have learned important lessons in life. As part of this book, I would like to share a few such life lessons with the readers, in the backdrop of a fictitious episode. As most of the incidents are based on one's life and their perception of things around them, I felt it wise to write in the first person as if the protagonist himself is narrating the story.

If any of you were able to relate any part of this story to your or someone's lives (which you should not, as I have not picked any incidents as they happened but made up an incident leading to the same result or learning), please dispose of the thought as a pure coincidence.

We all get dreams…Well, most of us! We dream about things that we like, things we hate, things we would want to do, things that we are scared of, things that we have seen in real life… What happens when we dream of something that we have never seen; when we see the same dream repeatedly; what if, it starts interfering with our lives? In this story, a person gets a dream about a temple. He ignores it initially but when it becomes recurrent, it starts bothering him in life. After a point, he starts believing in the existence of his dream and wants to chase it. What happens next forms the crux of the story.

Happy Reading!!!

Guru Prudhvi
Twitter: @guru_prudhvi

Acknowledgements

Dear readers,

Thank you from the bottom of my heart. The very fact that you are holding this book, speaks volumes about your support for a first-time author like me.

I would like to take a moment to thank my wife, Kiranmai who reviewed my book multiple times and helped me organise a huge pile of randomly written thoughts into a book that made sense.

Anil, Madan and Dasu annaiya (brother)! Thank you for being the first readers of my book and encouraging me with your feedback!

My parents - Thank you for taking care of me. I know you guys sacrificed your life for my upbringing. My daughters – Daya Dhaara and Dhwani – Thank you for bearing with me, especially towards the end of the book, when I had to spend the time of your share, on this book.

Lastly, I would like to thank the Almighty for giving me the wisdom to decide on writing this book.

-   Guru Prudhvi

Guru Prudhvi

I

I was seated in the car's rear seat looking out of the window, trying not to miss any of the scenic beauty as the car moved with difficulty on a steep curvy road, which seemed to end into the deep valley of pine trees at every bend and impulsively un-hide the next few yards of itself after the bend has been conquered. In a matter of a few minutes, the curvy road had transformed into a straight one as the car intentionally slowed down and eventually stopped at the foot of a hill. The driver signalled our arrival at the destination with a smile. When we got down, the first thing I noticed was the dense fog, which made the surroundings translucent. It took a few seconds for my eyes to adjust, to be able to figure out the backdrop. The next thing to be visible was a set of concrete stairs a few yards away from the place where I was standing which guided my sight to a building on the hilltop. By then, the driver had removed my suitcases from the trunk and handed over to me along with the bill. I paid him the money, thanked him and again set my eyes on the hilltop building, a chain of double storied row houses with cream exterior and brick-red roof.

My wife, carrying a bag in one hand and holding my daughter's hand with the other, started ascending the stairs slowly leaving me behind with the two suitcases. All my attempts to inspire myself to ascend the thirty-forty concrete steps with the two suitcases in my hand were put to rest when I saw a stout person in a maroon uniform rush down the stairs. He came close to me, greeted me with a nice smile and offered to carry my luggage. Before I could respond, he took the two suitcases from my hands and started climbing the stairs effortlessly as if it was a routine task for him. I followed him at my own slow pace, which was still good enough to overtake my wife and daughter, who were ascending at an even slower pace, thanks to my daughter's fear of height. While overtaking them, I took the bag from my wife to make her slow ascend easy and reached the entrance of the resort, approximately sixty-seconds after the stout guy. There I was greeted by another person who after seeing me pant, offered me to sit for a minute. When I sat on the sofa set waiting for my family to reach the reception area, I could see my two suitcases safely placed near the reception counter.

After completing the check-in formalities, we were escorted to the allotted room by the resort staff. The room was decently organised with a large king-sized bed, a wooden roof, a small sit-out and a gas room heater inside the room. We inspected the bathroom and we were satisfied with the condition. Then I opened the other door in the room, which led me to the sit-out. From the sit-out, I could see a breath-taking view of a large snow-clad mountain range at a distance with many green mountains and beautiful valleys on the way. The morning sun had just started glowing, which further enriched the view. After enjoying the view for a few seconds, I started inspecting the surroundings, which led my sight first to the barbed wire boundary fence of the resort a few yards away, and then to the winding trail, which started right from the edge of the fence and disappeared into the valley. The resort seemed to be strategically located for all tourists. My wife and daughter were still getting ready, which usually takes close to forty-five minutes. This allowed my adventurous self to take the front seat and explore the trail in the backyard. I went out of the hotel room and asked the receptionist for directions towards the trail before heading towards it.

I went down the trail admiring the tranquil beauty of nature. When I had walked for close to twenty minutes, I decided to head back. I took the exact path back but the resort was nowhere to be seen. I looked around for help but could not find anyone in the vicinity. That is when I heard the sound of a distant motor vehicle from one direction and I attempted to follow this lead to possibly find an inhabited area to seek help. When I reached the road, I found myself standing at the foot of another hill but no one was to be found. The hill was covered with very tall trees possibly pine. Right in front of me, I could see a white arch with something written on it, which I could not decipher. Beyond the arch, I could see endless staggered steps, which seem to have been made at the convenience of the mason, without the need to cut or dig the hill surface. I started climbing the steps and finally reached the top with the hope to find someone who could help me find my way back to the resort. The top of the hill was rather flat with fine stone flooring. I could see some more steps beside an asbestos shade. The shade had concrete racks in it. When I went up these steps, they led me to another arch, this time, a wooden one with a pointed top and another set of eight to ten stairs. On climbing these last set of steps, I was on a platform, which hosted an ancient-looking temple, but I could not recognise the deity inside. After offering respect to the deity, I went to explore the surroundings. The temple platform was surrounded by a fence. When I went towards the backside of the temple, I was astonished by the sight.

There was a huge chain of valleys, straight out of a Pixar animation movie, separated by different mountains. These valleys were coloured in various shades of green, brown and grey with occasional pink, orange and yellow coming from the flowers. Beyond the valley was an even better view of the ice-clad mountain range that I saw from my hotel room. I could hardly take off my eyes from the view when something caught my attention. The place where I was standing was a well-maintained garden with lawn and flower shrubs. There were clear pathways laid across the garden with occasional benches for visitors to sit and relax while enjoying the excellent view. I was so immersed in the beauty of nature that my eyes closed involuntarily and I forgot my purpose of existence for a few seconds. Then I mustered my senses and turned back towards the temple to find someone who could guide me back. On the way back to the temple, I saw that there was a huge rock that had a peculiar slanting shape as if it were from the NASA images of planet Mars. I went towards the rock and leaned forward as if to gauge the depth of the valley behind it. All of a sudden, I felt a strong push on my back and I slipped into the valley crying for help. I

opened my eyes in a state of shock and found myself lying on my bed and indeed, it was a push but
a mild one, by my wife, who was trying to wake
me up, to speak to my cousin who was on the
phone. I realised that it was a dream, again the
same dream!

I got up, sat on my bed and took the mobile phone
from my wife to speak to my cousin. My cousin,
Anil is a few years younger to me and we would
mostly interact using Social Media. Why did he call
so early in the morning? Is everyone doing fine? Is
there a problem? The moment, I heard his voice, I
could sense that there is no such problem and when
my mind, which was still half awake, started making sense of what he was speaking, I realised that it
was a piece of good news that he wanted to share.
Anil was getting married, that too, in two weeks!
My aunt wanted him to get married to his girlfriend before he travels to the States. Therefore, it
was celebration time for all of us.

My daughter had already ported all of us into the
castles of numerous princess stories that she knew
of and had started deciding on what everyone
should wear for the wedding. My wife and mom
were seriously debating on the wedding theme and
matching attire. My dad and I were silently listen-

ing. At least, my dad was! The celebration news and my family's excitement did little to distract my inner self from thoughts of the dream. I was thinking, *does such a place really exist? Can such a peaceful place really exist? If it does, I must definitely find it out. I must visit this place.*

This is how my journey started - a journey that would change my life forever!

-x-

II

As though the dream and the news of Anil's marriage were not enough to kick start my day with varied emotions, my office had its own flavours to add.

As usual, I entered my work-zone, walked to my desk and placed my laptop on it. As I plugged in one end of the power cable to the laptop and bent down to reach the plug point beneath the desk to plug in the other end of the cable, I heard a voice. It was Joshi, the peon of our zone who seconded as my boss' assistant. He brought the message of my boss who wanted me to stop by his cabin.

I work for Real Consulting Inc., often known as RCI, one of the premier software development and consulting firms in India. In my organisation, it is not rare to meet the boss. Hence, it appeared a mundane meeting but the fact, that my boss was in office ahead of me, was worthy of a suspicion which I ignored. I went to his cabin, knocked on the glass door twice, leaned opened the door and said,

"Good Morning Omkaar! You wanted to see me?"

"Hey Varun, come in. I have something for you." responded my boss in a concerned tone. Omkaar, my boss, was in a management role, due to which, he was allotted a cabin. His cabin was eight-by-eight feet in size and was made of glass partitions, which were frosted up to a height of around seven feet to make the room proceedings private.

Interestingly, Omkaar, at the time of his promotion, had insisted on occupying the cabin near the work-zone entrance so that he can keep an eye on the team. It was only later that we realised the actual reason for such a request. He did not want anyone to know when he comes and leaves the office!With these thoughts bringing a smile on my face, I went inside his cubicle and sat on the only vacant chair that was right in front of his desk. A few of my colleagues were already there in his room. Omkaar's boss, Arnab, was standing with his back rested against the counter shelf behind Omkaar's chair as if he was guiding him on something. Before I could say anything, Omkaar looked at me with a requesting face and said,

"Give me a minute, just drafting this urgent email. I'll get back to you"

I signalled 'ok' with a slight nod.It took him a few minutes to finish drafting the mail, after which, he turned back to check Arnab's reaction which was positive. He then looked towards me with an anxious smile, rotated his monitor screen towards me, and said,

"Read this email." I acknowledged and started reading the email that he had drafted,

"Dear Rick, We understand your concern. Our best associates have been put on this job since morning and one of them will be traveling tonight and reaching your head office by day after tomorrow. He will coordinate with all the stakeholders to get the situation under control. Please bear with us. Feel free to get back to me in case you need any further details.Cheers, Omkaar"

"Does that look fine? In case, you have not noticed, our CEO is on the copy list" Omkaar highlighted with a grin.

I immediately understood the reason for this short meeting so early in the morning but showed absolutely no expression on my face.

"Yes. I noticed that. It seems the Kool Look Corp. project is in a real mess." I could make out the client's name from the email addresses in the drafted email.

My organisation, Real Consulting Inc., was looking after the Information Technology operations of Kool Look Corp., one of our clients.

Omkaar nodded, "The CEO wants the very best to travel immediately. He wants an update every 2 hours. We are thinking of positioning you at their Head office in San Francisco for a few weeks"

The usual trick has been played with me, again. For the past eighteen months, Omkaar and Arnab have been sitting on my promotion and every time they find themselves in mess, they remember me as their 'best person'. This time, stakes were different. The CEO was involved. At the same time, I was in no mood to travel to the USA, especially when my cousin was getting married two weeks from now.

"The CEO is keeping a close eye on this. This will do wonders for your visibility within the organisation."

To hell with visibility! Where is my promotion? I wanted to scream."And your promotion will be cleared too," promised Arnab from the background as if he could read my mind.

"I can't travel now. My cousin is getting married in two weeks. I have to be here." I said in an assertive tone.

"You can come down for your cousin's wedding, all fares on the company" pleaded Omkaar in his typical way.I had to give in. The situation was sensitive and had I declined to go, I could have easily been projected as the reason for delays or failure.

My professional life was stable until a few years ago, until one day when something that I did became an instant hit within the organisation and I became a superstar in the office. That brought me a lot of visibility in management's eyes and since then, my life has been hell. On top of that, I have this 'great' quality of easily changing my personal plans and preferences for the sake of the organisation. I love my organisation, although I do not have any valid reasons for loving it. I joined this organisation, Real Consulting Inc., more than ten years ago, straight from my college campus. I never explored any job opportunities outside and never even created a good CV. I have a very good name in the organisation and have been in a very good role but that's about it. I am underpaid, easily manipulated and over-utilised. Most of the time, I try to find positives out of such manipulations and adjust myself.

This time was no different and my brain had already started persuading me to accept this as an opportunity to shop for the wedding in San Francisco. After agreeing to go, I came out of Omkaar's cubicle and immediately called my wife, Karishma to tell her about my travel the same night.

"Karishma, I have to travel to the United States tonight. One of our clients escalated some issues to our CEO and they need me there."

"How long will you be gone?" asked my wife

"About two weeks."

"Are you sure, you will be back before Anil's wedding?"

"Yes, Of Course! That was my condition before agreeing."

"Oh. ok. Will you be carrying the same suitcase that you took to Malaysia last month? Should I pack it? What time is your flight? And which place are you going this time?"

"I don't have the tickets yet. I'll be going to the Bay Area. The Malaysia suitcase is fine."

Usually, whenever I call my wife from office, the conversation would be very robotic and to the point. Especially, if they are about my ad-hoc business trips! Informing our five-year-old daughter was the hardest thing to do and that would put the two of us, off. My daughter would, in most cases, think that I am going on a trip to punish her for not eating food or crying. On hearing about my trip, she would come to me and plead me not to go, promising me that she would behave well. We always fail to understand, how and why she correlates my trips with her own behaviour.

After my daughter returned from school, my wife told her that I was going to the US for the wedding shopping and promised her a princess frock. Thankfully, she bought that idea and did not feel that bad. My wife had called me up to inform me, as she was aware that I would be worried.

The next few hours in office were spent with the Kool Look Corp. offshore team who knew the entire history that caused this mess. I had a few questions, which I tried to find answers for, before leaving for the war zone, the head office in San Francisco.My tickets, forex, and other documents were ready by 4 pm, which I collected from the travel administration department before leaving for home.

By the time I reached home, Karishma had already packed my suitcase, prepared dinner for me, informed the driver to drop me at the airport and notified Sravan about my trip to San Francisco. Sravan, our common friend, stayed in San Francisco and was to receive me at the airport.

She is super-efficient. How can she remember all these things?

I had an early dinner with my family and left for the airport by 8 pm. I checked in my luggage and opted for a window seat. No matter how many times I fly, I always cherish the sight of the landscape underneath while flights take off, especially at night. I feel as if 'Google Earth' has a night version and I am zooming it out.

-x-

III

I boarded the flight and sunk in the cramped economy seat. The economy seats were a big pain in my butt, literally; thanks to my hefty body structure which, for my height, makes the BMI swing between very fat and slightly obese. I had to spend the next twenty-plus hours in such a seat; hence wanted to come to terms with it. With such a thought, I wore the sterilised eye mask that was provided by the air hostess and tried to catch a few hours of sleep.

There were multiple visuals competing inside my mind to occupy the majority of the thoughts. It was the face of my five-year-old daughter, who won the mind battle first. I could remember her 'almost' crying face when I had to spend my evening on teleconferences for my office arrangements at San Francisco while she was hoping that I would take her out for cycling as per my promise the day before. Moreover, the fact that she will not see me for the next two weeks had started to bother her. As I remembered her face, I felt very bad for my general behaviour towards her. Most of the time, when she would come to me for something, I would be busy; and would even vent out my office misery at her on simple things which would make her cry. Her cry would further exacerbate things, as that would catalyse my misery with the guilt that I had shouted at her and would result in threatening her to stop crying.

She is just five. Why do I behave like a stupid and shout at her as if she is a grown-up adult?

The next item to occupy my mind was my misery in the office where I was trying to succeed while still trying to figure out what success really means. My mind has been so fluctuating between demanding a lavish comfortable life with a good career and, opting for a simple lifestyle doing something very simple and spending quality time with family. Whenever the mind turned towards simplistic life, the future planning, inflation, my current liabilities and my good record of accomplishment during academics would take precedence, digressing me away from the thoughts of leaving the corporate life. When the mind wanders into the depth of the career opportunities and I look at my role models in this path, some other part of the mind takes the control and asks me questions like *what are you gaining out of this? Will you be happy to retire rich and not being able to spend time with family? Are the personal sacrifices of your role models justified with their career success?*

Before I could think further, my chain of thought was interrupted by a friendly greeting.

"How do you do?"

When I took off my eye mask, I noticed that on the very next seat was an aged person, should be in his late sixties, who introduced himself as Mr. Mahapatra. I could not grasp his first name but was reluctant to ask him again. To his left was his wife. The duo told me that they were traveling to Seattle to meet their son who worked over there. While Mr. Mahapatra was keen on talking to me, I still had multiple things going on in my mind ranging from the plan to clear the mess in the office, my daughter and wife, my cousin's marriage and my dream. Hence, I was responding disinterestedly to all his queries until he realised that I am not interested in speaking and he himself kept quiet.

I had just closed my eyes for a nap when the Airhostess woke me up for dinner. I was feeling hungry due to the early dinner and took the serving.

On opening it, I saw some non-vegetarian food on my plate. I requested the air hostess for a replacement as I am a staunch vegetarian for which she responded in negative quoting that she will have to wait till everyone is done to check if she is left with any extra vegetarian food. I was cursing my fate and the airline when Mr. Mahapatra offered his vegetarian food to me.

He said, "Son, we take non-vegetarian food but had ordered vegetarian. We can exchange our meals if you prefer to."

I felt bad, as I did not behave well with him during our chat earlier. However, on his insistence, we exchanged our meals.

After finishing the meal, I apologised to him, "Sorry sir, my mind was a bit occupied when we last spoke."

"I can understand, son. My son is a software engineer too." He laughed.

"So… are you visiting the US for the first time?", I wanted to continue the talk. So asked randomly whatever came in my mind.

"No. I have a green card. I stayed in the US for five years and returned to India. Now I spend a few months a year in the US and remaining in India"

"Interesting! I believe you are a retired person. Otherwise, it is difficult to plan things in a favourable way."

Mr. Mahapatra smiled, "It is not like that. I never parked any of my plans for retirement. It is not worth it. I lived all my dreams before I retired. Now I am living as per the plans of my children."

I was stunned.

He continued, "Life is like that. For the initial twenty odd years, you live your parents' dreams and after sixty, you live your children's dreams, not because they interfere with your life, but because you want to live with them and are too old to execute your own plans all by yourself. You still have your own forty years to live your life between twenty and sixty!"

I found logic in his words but was curious on how to shape those forty years in your own favour. So I intervened, "But Sir, aren't those forty years meant to build and save your future?"

"That is partially true. At least that is what we are made to believe by our parents who are too worried about our future and are not willing to let go of us."

"Son", he continued with a firm tone, "are you interested in this topic?"

I nodded.

He continued, "Let me explain to you the concept of Black Swan, which governs our lives more than we think. There is something called a Positive Black Swan, which indicates a situation in one's life where he becomes successful within a short time, mostly dictated by a single event. For Ex: getting the first break in movies, music album or a book becoming a best seller, getting successful in business instantly, etc. This is what most youngsters aim for."

"True. Even I wanted to become a sportsperson during my teens. Even today, I feel that I am good at singing and can make a career out of it."

He smiled, "But, most youngsters do not even give themselves a chance to attain Positive Black Swan, due to the worries of parents or the insecurities associated with Positive Black Swan. The cause of such worries is the Negative Black Swan, which indicates a situation that is just reverse of Positive Black Swan. A situation or a moment, which makes a person lose everything and hit the low in life. For Ex: losing one's job and not being able to get another one, crashing of one's business, losing vital organs needed for the job, etc."

"It is ghastly even to think about." I was feeling anxious already.

"This is what most parents worry about. About their children, hitting the negative black swan! They are very concerned about giving their kids a stable and settled lifestyle which will ensure that they never land upon a negative black swan."

My childhood memories started flashing in front of me. Every time, I picked up my hockey stick, my dad would be terrified and would get a headache. I could remember one particular incident when I had to skip the selections event, as my dad did not seem happy about me trying to become a sportsperson. I was too sincere to go against his happiness, even though he would not express it in words. I could never forget the way in which his eyes would light up when I did well in academics and always felt that it was the best gift and motivation for me to perform even better in academics.

My train of thought was interrupted by Mr. Mahapatra's words, "Do you know, apart from parents, there is another category of people who worry about the negative black swan?"

I was confused.

He continued, "Youngsters, who are mature and intelligent!"

"Aah. Interesting! This probably explains why intelligent kids in school do not usually make it large. They are too worried to take risks and try to save the negative black swan throughout their life." My mind was running at a speed faster than the flight in which we were seated. I could think of numerous examples of famous personalities who were not intelligent and those classmates from school who would struggle to even get passing grades in the exams but were very successful entrepreneurs today.

Mahapatra nodded with a smile.

"Sir, tell me more about your own journey during those forty years which were your own", I wanted to take leads from his life to live my life the way I wanted to but, that is when I realised that, it was getting late and the aged man needed some rest. So I changed my question, "Sir, there is a lot to learn from you. Can I be in touch with you while you are in the US or once you are back in India?"

"Sure, Son. This is my visiting card with my address and contact numbers. You can drop in anytime. But…", he stopped midway to drink water and continued, "But, you need to look within your own self to understand what you want to do with those forty years."

After an elongated pause, probably waiting for me to say something, he said, "What are you searching for? Where do you want to go? What are your dreams? What gives you happiness? Think and look within."

I was still silent, deep in my thoughts finding answers to these questions when he realised that I would need some time and said, "Good Night Son. We will speak more about this when we meet next."

"Good Night Sir!", I was not going to sleep that night or rather a day; I didn't know what to address that time as; as we had already hopped through multiple time zones during the flight.

I took the visiting card in my hand. It read, "Dr. Anurag Mahapatra, M. Sc., M. Phil, D.Sc." and had his address. Thankfully I didn't have to go through the embarrassment of asking him for his first name. *He is actually 'Dr. Mahapatra'. But he did not introduce himself as a Doctor. Maybe, he was too humble to call himself a Doctor!*

After Mr. Mahapatra slept, I was still wondering about what he told me about the personal forty years and the concept of Black Swan. My life so far was starting to make sense. I could see a logical flow throughout. My mind had already been set on the right direction! These positive thoughts seemed to have brought the necessary calmness in my mind, which helped me to sleep for a few hours unknowingly, and when I woke up, the flight was already getting closer to New York, our port of entry to the United States.

The Mahapatras would take a flight to Seattle from New York and I would take a different flight to San Francisco.

After the flight landed in New York, we greeted each other and I promised to call him up and meet him once he was back in India.

On my flight to San Francisco, I was still thinking about the questions that Mr. Mahapatra had asked me. I was still not sure of the answers but I was no longer feeling cheated by life for not being as successful as others were.

During my college days, I was told by a professor that I could opt to do anything that I wish to do and I will be successful there; that I need not constrain myself to do something traditional. Anything I would choose to do, I would succeed. He told me this after he had apparently given a challenge to the entire class on a surprise test to score more than six out of twenty and I was the only one to win that challenge and I had actually scored twenty out of twenty.

I was always a topper even in my school. All my teachers used to tell me that I have immense will power, which is capable of taking me to unexplored heights. At the age of eleven, when I got my IQ tested, I was told that I have the intelligence of an eighteen-year-old. Even at school, I was always told that I am very mature and I usually found matching frequencies in senior classes, rather than in my own class.

Was this the reason that I never took risks or never ever tried to do what my heart wanted me to do? Is this why, I act as if I love my organisation, while at the depth of my mind, I am just scared to change my job and am insecure due to the fear of negative black swan?

I landed at San Francisco airport with these questions in my mind. After I had collected my baggage, I stepped out of the airport to find Sravan standing in front of me with a big smile. I had met him a few months ago at his wedding in Hyderabad.

I, Sravan and Karishma were together in school. Sravan now works for Google in Bay Area while his wife, Priya is a homemaker. We spoke about the good old days in school on our way back to his home. He stayed in the Redwood City area which was a few miles away from San Francisco but was very close to the Kool Look Corp. Head office.

We had a nice dinner, which was cooked by Priya. After the dinner, Sravan insisted on me staying with him since the office was very close by which I politely declined. However, I promised to come over to his house every weekend and wanted to stay at the hotel during the weekdays. I was sure that I will have to work late and it would cause hassles to the newly married couple.

The next morning, I went to the office from Sravan's house along with my baggage. It was a very hectic day but I somehow managed to get out of office by 7 pm and checked into the hotel right across the street. While in the hotel, I had a good amount of time to retrospect my life so far but had little success in finding answers. The entire week passed by at an express speed as if the clock was ticking thrice as faster.

Friday morning, I received a call from Sravan, "Dude, I'll pick you at 6 from your office. Is the time fine?"

"Sravan, let's make it at 7 pm but meet me at the hotel and we'll have dinner at my hotel. Their salads are awesome. You will like them. Bring along Priya too."

"If it is for Salads, I am ever ready. See you at 7"

Sravan and Priya, as usual, were dot on time in reaching the hotel. I had just returned from the office and was packing my luggage for checkout to save on two days of hotel charges when I would be away. This was part of the guidelines given at Real Consulting Inc., which was rarely followed by the employees, but I had religiously followed it, after all, I loved my organisation; at least, that is what I thought.

After I packed my luggage, we went downstairs to the restaurant, which served Salad buffet as dinner. Although there were numerous varieties of Salads, they had pizzas, pasta, cakes, etc., for people like me who are fond of 'calories'.

All through the dinner, we spoke about many things from our old days, our friends, hometown, etc., and some particular topics of special interest to Priya – our infatuations and girlfriends. During our conversations, Priya would get excited about show-ing me the Golden Gate, Half Moon Bay, Pier 39, etc., and every time, Sravan had to remind her that I had stayed for three years in the Bay area and had seen them all. We had a fun time and did not realise that the clock had struck eleven by the time we started from the restaurant.

It was already late, so I went to bed straightaway. We had planned to visit Gilroy the next day so that I can do my shopping for the wedding. Gilroy was close to sixty miles from Sravan's home and was famous for factory outlets of every famous brand I have ever known. I had planned to purchase a good watch for my cousin and some good jeans and shirts for myself. My daughter had told me to buy a princess frock for her. I was thinking about all this while sleeping.

That night, I again had the same dream. The same hotel, temple, and the view! It again ended with someone pushing me hard into the valley. However, this time, there was no one pushing me in reality. Nevertheless, I woke up suddenly scared of falling down. I could not sleep after that. I was awake trying to find clues from the dream to find the places that I saw. While I was getting frustrated for not being able to find any temples, which resembled the one in my dream, my crazy office laptop was equally contributing to my frustration by getting rebooted every ten minutes. I finally gave up and tried searching for brands in Gilroy using my mobile phone.

The next morning, I was not my usual self and Sravan was very quick to notice that. As I was sipping my coffee, Sravan asked me, "Dude, what are you thinking about?"

"Nothing serious buddy"

"No, something is troubling you."

"It's just the dream. I saw a dream in which I visit an ancient-looking temple and in the backdrop, I can see a beautiful view of ice-clad mountains and flowery valleys."

"ok…"

"I saw the exact same dream five times in the last three months. And… it ends with someone pushing me into the valley."

"and…"

"And I want to find that temple out and visit that place."

"Dude, do you really believe that such a place exists? And even if it exists, what on earth makes you feel that you want to visit that place?"

"I truly believe that such a place exists. And I am mesmerised by the sheer beauty of that place."

"Varun, listen to me. You are an educated person. You should know that dreams reflect your own self."

"Sravan, I know that. And that is exactly why I want to visit that place. To understand what my dream wants to convey? In reality, I don't know what I want to do. I have spent years in the same organisation, fooling myself that I am happy here. But not anymore! This dream has given me a lead to find my destiny."

"If you really want to understand and interpret your dream, I can help you with that. One of my friends at Stanford is doing his research on Dream Interpretation. We can meet him tomorrow. Let us try to find answers scientifically instead of running behind the dream aimlessly."

"Dream Interpretation! What is that?"

"Yes. It is a research area related to psychology. This research helps individuals understand what they really want by interpreting their dreams over a period of time."

"Great! I wasn't aware that such a thing exists"

"Let me speak to my friend; his name is Pallav. I'll fix a time for tomorrow."

"Excellent!"

"Now get ready. We need to go for your shopping."

I felt relaxed as well as enthusiastic as I was going to know what my dream means, finally. That too, without the need to search for the temple or visiting it!

I took my bath and had my breakfast. Priya had prepared some good sprouts parathas (Indian bread) with mint dressing. I liked those so much that I called up Karishma and made her learn the recipe from Priya.

We started for Gilroy around 11 am. Sravan took the highway 101 directly to Gilroy. During the drive, Sravan had put his iPod in random shuffle mode and we were playing the guessing game on what could the next song be. At one instance, one of our favourites, the song, 'Naadaan Parindey' started playing. We stopped our game and started enjoying the song. The song compares people with the nomadic birds, which travel all the way from their homes to different continents for food, water and fun and how the birds have to reach home to be complete. This song took me back to two years ago when I was staying in San Jose with my wife and daughter. We were having a good life with all the comforts. Our parents used to visit us once a year and we would visit them once. We would have a video call once a week and a daily phone call. We were able to save some money so that our future is secure. In one instance, we could not go to India and my parents visited us after a gap of eighteen months. When we went to the airport to receive my parents, we realised that my parents are getting old. This song had released around the same time and had played a catalyst in reminding us of my motherland, INDIA and what I was missing by staying back in the United States.

But today, when I was listening to this song with my eyes closed, all I could see is our rented apartment in San Jose, the adjoining park, my daughter's school in the US, my office in the US, the Indian shop, the downtown and the relaxed lives in the US. There was not even a single instance when I shouted on my daughter or was dull. The song unexpectedly started having a reverse effect on me from what it had in the past. I was suddenly feeling that I am missing the United States!

I told Sravan that on our way back, we need to visit San Jose. He agreed. In fact, he himself wanted to take his wife to a particular restaurant in San Jose, which was our favourite.

Soon, we reached Gilroy and parked our car in the '108 Outlet' zone parking and went into the shops one by one. It was a common practice to first do window-shopping to understand the deals and discounts available. On that particular day, we found good deals in US Polo Assn., Sketchers, and Levis. I got myself a pair of Jeans, four T-shirts, a pair of Sketchers Shape up shoes and a US Polo Watch for my cousin. For my wife, I took two pairs of Jeans, which I measured against the sample that I carried from India (A pat on my own back). But we couldn't find the princess dress that my daughter wanted.

It was close to 2 pm by the time we were done with my shopping and all of us were hungry. As we had decided to go to our favourite restaurant in San Jose for lunch, Sravan took Highway 101 and took the highway 880 exit to visit our favourite Restaurant "Dee Dee's". It is an Indian specialty restaurant, which served one authentic north Indian cuisine per week. That week, it was Gujarati food. We had the best Gujarati food ever, even better than the one we get in India and were extremely full to drive back immediately. So we went around San Jose downtown which was our usual meeting point when I was in the Bay Area a few years ago.

We also went to Macy's where I finally found the princess dress that my daughter wanted.

We sat in the park for some time, went to Starbucks before starting for home. It was a fun day shopping in the morning and a nostalgic one in the afternoon.

I miss the US. This is what I had thought through-out the afternoon.

We reached home late and had ordered Pizza on the way back. We enjoyed our dinner at home, con-tinuing our chat from the previous day at the restaurant.

-x-

IV

The next day was an important day for me. I was going to speak to a psychologist friend of Sravan, who was doing research in dream interpretation. And I was hoping to find what I really want.

Sravan had already spoken to Pallav and we were to meet him around 3 pm in the Stanford Cafeteria.

Stanford University was around twenty minutes' drive from Sravan's place. The plan was to start after lunch.

We had a loaded lunch that day, with Priya trying to feed me with everything she knew the recipe of. We started for Stanford around 2 pm as I was worried about not reaching on time. Sravan kept on telling me that it is not a formal appointment as Pallav is a dear friend. But I insisted on starting early, even though I knew Sravan's habit of reaching on time, always.

We reached Stanford around 2:30 pm and went to the cafeteria. Sravan informed Pallav about it and we hardly had to wait for a few mins before Pallav was in front of us.

Pallav was a tall fat guy who would be in his early thirty's just like us and was very cheerful.

He started formally with a firm shake hand but within a few mins, he was moving very closely and giving me the same comfortable feeling. I thought *Psychologists need to be like him to be able to help their clients.*

After the initial general talk, we came to the point.

Pallav asked, "So Varun, Sravan told me that you want to speak to me"

"Yes, Pallav. I need your help to gain some clarity on a slice of my life, especially pertaining to a recurring dream, which I have been seeing since the last few months."

"Can you tell me the dream in detail? And while you do so, please explain the way you see it, not your interpretations. Is that going to be ok?"

I nodded with a nervous smile.

"So it goes like this…." And I explained to him the entire dream.

"Pallav, yesterday was the fifth time that I got the same dream in the last few months"

"Interesting. Was it exactly the same every time?"

"Yes, it was. Every time, I see the same hotel, same temple and the same scenic view from behind the temple and the same push into the valley."

"Wow!" exclaimed Pallav and continued, "Let me try to understand. You see a hotel, mountains, valleys, flowers, stairs, taxi, temple, rocks, and benches. And it ends with someone pushing you into the valley. The valley looks beautiful from the top, but obviously, no one wants to fall into it." He was seriously trying to understand the dream and at the same time, his humour was unstoppable and probably the way he connected to his clients.

I nodded.

"We have been doing some good amount of research on Dream Interpretation. What we usually do is to try and correlate a person's dreams with his past, present situations, his aspiration, ambitions and mental state. We have created predictive models that can reverse-engineer the situation, desire or mental state based on the dreams one sees."

"Fantastic", was my reaction, "So, what would my dream reveal?"

"Before we go there, let me ask you a few more questions. Have you been to any hill station in the past?"

"Yes. I have been to some hill stations, but none resemble even remotely to what I see in my dreams. I have seen ice-clad mountains but none resemble those."

"Ok. Do you get a sense of déjà vu when you think about the locations that you saw in your dreams? Maybe, you saw those in some televisions shows or movies?"

"Hmm. I don't think so. While the locations look fresh in my mind, I don't think I saw them ever in real life. I even searched the internet with all the popular hill stations in India and every other country where an Indian temple could probably exist. By the way, I forgot to mention that it was an Indian temple for sure based on the structure that I can remember. All I could know from the internet-based research is that the snow-clad mountain ranges appear to be the Himalayas. If you could help me interpret my dream, it would be really helpful." I had already started to sound desperate.

"Varun, dreams are nothing but a reflection of mental state, fears, aspirations, etc. From our analysis, each object that you saw in your dream signifies something. We have applied this model and were able to successfully map to real-life scenarios. This method has helped numerous people in understanding what they really want to do with their life. Especially, those who are confused with their job, education, line of study, etc. get benefited. While this is not a sure shot method and there are exceptions, if you promise that you will stop chasing this dream once you understand the details and get back to normal self, I can share the results of interpretation of the sight of objects in your dream."

"Pallav, I promise. I just want to decode this dream and put an end to my curiosity in this regard."

"Ok. So let's get started." Pallav pulled out his MacBook and started feeding some information into an application and said, "First of all, you saw a taxi. A taxi generally signifies a desire to go for a vacation or the fact that you are being taken for a ride at the office or home. You also saw a bench, which symbolises the need to take rest."

"Pallav, this seems to be spot on. We have been trying to go for a vacation for the last 18 months. But due to a lot of unplanned events and office pressure, the plan had to be postponed numerous times. Both I and my wife are desperately looking for a break from the normal routine."

He continued, "Stairs normally indicate elevation, either physically, mentally, spiritually, financially or socially. It may even indicate a phase of transition. Hotels indicate a temporary place to stay. From both stairs and hotel, the common interpretation is the state of transition. Does this ring any bells?"

"Hmm... I am not sure if I am in a state of transition. But yes, I am in a confused state of mind, especially from my career front. I was always a topper in school and was in the top 10% in college and a 9-pointer in post-graduation. Any project, big or small; any task, relevant to my skills or not; I was always successful. I have done really hard work since my childhood, sacrificed my hobbies which I could have turned into my career. And for the last few years, I feel that my growth has stagnated. I do not like the work I am doing. I feel that I am overqualified for my job. I have seen people, who enjoyed their childhood and college and were just good enough to be promoted to the next class. And today, I find myself either working with them at the same level or find that I am earning much lesser than what they are earning. I feel that I have gained nothing out of all this hard work and minor sacrifices that I did so far."

I continued with the inputs from Mahapatra uncle's words, "Probably, I was too-mature-too-early to take major risks and always chose a safe path in life. But I think, I have to find solace somewhere."

"Nobody likes their own job. Every person has a low period. Just stick around and knowing you, I don't see a reason why you wouldn't excel." said Pallav in a concerned tone and continued, "Mountains indicate obstacles and valleys indicate your vulnerabilities and the need to be protected."

"Ok. What about the temple?" I was getting impatient due to the fact that a lot of the interpretations that Pallav was explaining were fitting my current situation.

"Temple may represent your spiritual desires or a place for you to attain peace."

"Hmmm. So in all, what do you think of the entire dream? What do you suggest to your clients in such cases?" I was all pumped up.

Pallav bent forward, raised his eyebrows and steadily looked into my eyes and said in a flat, soft tone, "Varun, your dream is not uncommon. Overall, it indicates the need for you to take a break from your routine life. Just go for a holiday and relax. Once you are in a stable mood, think over your priorities and plan your action. And please, forget about this dream."

I was in agreement with the overall interpretation and the suggestion given by Pallav and I had made up my mind to follow it fully.

I thanked Pallav for all the help and went back to Sravan's home. The next morning, Sravan dropped me at my office and left for his office.

The incidents over the weekend had a very positive effect on me. The escalated issues at Kool Look Corp. were already getting on track and my personal satisfaction had further helped me to take a very positive approach towards work. While the initial plan was for me to take a few days off for my cousin's marriage and return to the US after that, with things coming back on track, my boss was confident that I will not need to return to the US after my cousin's marriage. Instead, he had planned to visit the US in such a way that there is an overlap before I leave.

On the day of the journey, my boss, Omkaar was already in office. We had a couple of handover meetings and status checkpoints. I started early from the office and went to the hotel. I finished packing my baggage which was augmented by an additional big suitcase which I had to purchase to accommodate the shopping that included chocolates, dried berries, energy bars, clothes, and whatnot.

Sravan dropped me at the airport on time. I checked in and boarded the flight. This time, on the next seat, was a beautiful lady in her twenties who was going back to India to get married. We had a few common topics and spoke briefly and casually. I am not sure if I flirted with her, but had really no intention to do so as I was dying to get back home.

The flight landed on time at the Rajiv Gandhi International Airport in Hyderabad. I took a cab and went home. My wife and daughter were eagerly waiting for me. It was a fun time with my family after close to two weeks.

I also called up my cousin to inform about my return and to check the progress on the wedding planning. The wedding was planned in Hyderabad itself, at my cousin's farmhouse. Most of our relatives were to arrive the following day and some of them were to be stationed at my home too for a day before we all went to the farmhouse together. So I checked with him on the timings and other details so that arrangements could be made accordingly. However, my wife had already taken care of all those things.

I should have known. This is what I thought when my wife told me from behind that all arrangements are made.

-x-

V

My wife and I were busy with the wedding arrangement. Both of us had applied for a week-long leave. I had deliberately not told anyone else about my dream as it would unnecessarily open up some of the thoughts that were bothering me in my life. In addition, the chapter of that dream was closed as per my promise to Pallav.

But that night, I got the same dream again. This time, I saw something else too. After ascending the concrete stairs that led to the hilltop, I could see a queue of devotees holding something in their hand. When I followed the line towards the front, I could see a priest standing and taking the offering from the devotee, while uttering some verses at a very high speed. The priest had his head shaved off, except for a small ponytail at the centre of his head. He was just wearing a saffron cloth, which was tied from his loin and was just long enough to cover his knee. I went closer to the priest and tried to understand what was going on. The devotees were, in fact, offering "crowns" to the deity. Some of the crowns were made of metal while most of them were made of clay and painted with different colours. The priest was taking the crowns, one at a time, placing them on the idol of God and then making a pile behind him. When the priest saw me, he smiled at me and asked me to help him dispose of the crowns. Even before I could respond, he kept a pile of crowns on my head and asked me to discard those in the valley behind the temple.

As I walked with half a dozen crowns on my head, I could see a large number of people gathered around me, assembled in a line on either side of the path to the backside of the temple that leads to the valley, with folded hands with a sense of respect in their eyes! I slowly walked past the temple and started to dispose of the crowns into the valley, one at a time. When I was about to dispose of the last crown, I could hear a huge roar from the gathering. I turned towards the crowd and everyone was waving at me. Suddenly, the rock on which I was standing to dispose of the crowns started sliding and I fell into the valley.

I woke up with anxiety, only to find everything normal, except for my heartbeat. I immediately opened my laptop and started typing an email to Pallav.

"Dear Pallav,

How are you doing? I got the same dream again. This time, I also saw a crown being offered to the deity. Later, the offered crowns were put on my head by the priest and I was asked to dispose of them in the valley. Everyone was offering respect to me in my dream. Can you help me with the significance of this?

Warm Regards,

Varun"

Almost instantly, I got a response:

"Dear Varun,

Crowns represent thoughts or power. The feeling of being respected by others or placing the crown on your head could indicate that you are not being respected in real life or not getting the due credit for your effort. While we can speak and discuss the intricate details of your dream, which will help me in improving my research on dreams, I would not want to do that as I have seen people go crazy behind the dreams and I do not want you to do so. Hence, please stop chasing that dream.

Regards,

Pallav"

While I appreciated Pallav's response, my mind was still full of questions. Does the temple of my dreams really exist? If yes, where is it? Why am I getting additional hints regarding the temple? I am sure there would not be many temples where crowns are offered to the deity. I opened my laptop and started searching the internet. I tried searching with keywords like 'temple where a crown is offered', 'deity crown temple', 'temple near hill station' etc. but all I could find were articles pertaining to some celebrity who offers crowns to different temples in Southern India. And there were no temples in Southern India that resembled the one in my dream.

The dream had again started bothering me. I was getting desperate to find the whereabouts of this temple and visit it.

- x -

VI

It is common in our community to celebrate a wedding for three days. There were different events and rituals to be performed throughout the three days which would leave everyone including the couple-to-be extremely exhausted. Normally, the wedding function would take place in the bride's hometown. But the bride and groom were both from Hyderabad and my uncle insisted that the three-day wedding program be held at my cousin's farmhouse which was huge by any standards. My uncle, a college dropout, had shifted to Hyderabad more than forty years ago and had invested in real estate wisely. That yielded great returns and now he was a billionaire and had a huge farmhouse in the not-so-outskirts of the city. My dad, on the other hand, joined Railways after his engineering and had to travel all over the country. While he was respected throughout his service, he could not save a lot but just enough to lead a sufficient middle-class life.

The farmhouse had a big swimming pool, a Barbeque area, a children's play area, a mini theatre, a couple of fountains and some artificial waterfalls and water bodies with small wooden bridges on it. There was a small stage behind the swimming pool and an open area capable of seating close to two hundred people where the key functions were to be organised. There were twelve rooms each sufficient to accommodate six adults and two dormitories with fifty beds each. Hence a majority of close friends and family were staying in the farmhouse itself. Others were placed in hotels nearby. It was mandatory for every guest, irrespective of the fact whether he is staying in the farmhouse or outside, to have all meals right from breakfast until supper at the farmhouse. That would mean that everyone was at the farmhouse from 7 am until 11 pm at least and it was a festive atmosphere with almost every-one participating in all the functions.

I too was an active participant in most of the func-tions, but on the day of the wedding, I had also in-vited my close friends – Vinay and Sapan. The three of us were together in college and had a great grand time together. We would not shy away from any adventures and would encourage each other in every useless thing right from proposing a girl to bunking classes. Although all three of us were stay-ing in the same city, we could hardly meet. Hence, I had decided that I will try to relive those college days when I meet them at my cousin's wedding.

When they came to the farmhouse, I was the one who received them and after the regular formalities of blessing the bride and bridegroom and getting blessed by my parents, the three of us sat by the poolside with cola in our hands and started talking about various things. Then we started competing on the weirdest things that happened to us in the last few months. Vinay, now a government official at the Secretariat had seen his supervisor getting slapped on his face. Sapan, a software engineer like me, and a father of two kids, was proposed by his subordinate, thinking that he is single. Now was my turn.

"Guys, I had a dream", I wanted to share my dream incident with them as that was one of the weirdest things that ever happened to me. At the same time, I had some hope that the duo will be able to help me find the temple.

"What is so weird about it?", joked Sapan, "I get dreams every day."

"Listen baba." Said a curious Vinay

I continued, "And the dream repeats itself. I at least saw the same dream thrice in the last week itself."

"And…" Vinay's curiosity was increasing exponentially.

"It is about me visiting a temple." And I narrated the entire dream to them including the latest addition of crown donation sequence.

Then I expressed my desire to find the temple and visit it.

"So you want to go there and wait for someone to come and push you in the valley," said Sapan with a vicious smile as if he wanted to come and push me.

"Do you want to do that honour?" I said.

"Definitely. But I don't see any valley here but I can do this" and he acted as if he is trying to push me into the swimming pool.

"Guys, I am serious. I really want to find that temple. Would you help me find it?"

"Sure Varun. I have some contacts in the tourism ministry and will try to find the temple." As Vinay said this, he turned towards Sapan and told him, "Your in-laws are very spiritual right? They keep taking these trips to remote temples in the Himalayas right? Why don't you ask them too?"

"I don't speak to my in-laws normally. But will do it for our friendship." He was obviously overacting. "But please, don't ask me to accompany you. I am least interested in temples. Moreover, I can't see you falling into the valley… sob…sob…"

That day we had a great time together after so many years. They left for home after the wedding. The next day was the last day of the endless functions of the wedding after which, we all started and reached home. It was a Friday and I was thankful that I would at least get two days of solid rest before getting grilled at the office starting Monday.

-x-

VII

I joined the office after a weeklong leave. I was feeling rejuvenated after the break and was hopeful of getting the promotion that I deserved as promised by Arnab, my boss' boss if I traveled to the US for the Kool Look Corp. escalation. It was just a week ago that I had led the team from the front to handle that escalation and had earned a good reputation from the customer.

I went to my cubicle and connected my laptop which I did not even open in the last few days. I had not even checked my mails during my break.

I hated it when someone on leave would connect to the office to behave as if they are irreplaceable. *I would never do that.*

There were close to two hundred unread emails in my mailbox; a third of those from Kool Look Corp. customer. There was one email forwarded by Arnab to me with the subject 'Team Restructure'. I was excited as I was expecting to be promoted. One promotion would put me into the Management Organisation Structure as Omkaar.

I opened the email and was shocked to note that the promotion that I deserved was actually given to Omkaar. Omkaar now was leading an additional team. My name was nowhere in the organisation structure. Bottom Line: I was not promoted and was still reporting to Omkaar and was stuck in the same role.

I stood up from my seat and stormed into Arnab's cabin. "Arnab, I want to talk to you about something."

"Please sit down", said Arnab with a question mark face.

"You promised me. I went to the US, handled the escalation for the organisation. But I have not been promoted."

"Varun, we could not promote two associates at the same time in the team. And Omkaar had handled the situation very well at the US after you returned." Arnab was multitasking. He was staring at his laptop, having coffee and speaking to me. His eyes were stuck at his laptop, probably; his conscience did not allow him to look into my eyes. He continued in the same poise, "Even the customer had very good words to say about Omkaar and not even a single appreciation for you."

"Come On Arnab! Everyone knows that Omkaar only visited the US towards the end of the escalation, at a point when everything was almost settled. I was on the line of fire for close to two weeks and I was instrumental in bringing things back on track."

"There is a difference between 'almost' and 'complete'. You left it midway and gave preference to your personal issues. Omkaar, on the other hand, left on the day of his child's birthday."

I was surprised to hear this bullshit from Arnab. I really felt that the two of us don't belong to the same place.

I stood up, without saying a word, walked back to my cubicle, closed my laptop, and headed for home.

I am going to leave this organisation.

People do not leave organisations. They leave their immediate supervisors. This is what I was told during my management training. Very true!

I was all pumped up to leave the organisation but when I reached home and thought in the calmness of my bathtub, I felt that I should continue in the same organisation at least for a few months. The promotion that I was expecting was a big one. It would increase my salary by close to forty percent.

No other organisation would give me this hike. Let me first take a few weeks' break. I should not take any decisions in haste.

I applied for a three-week vacation and got it approved by Omkaar. Omkaar was more than happy to approve my vacation, as he did not want any hurdles for the first few days in the new role. I could think of the Black Swan concept that Mr. Mahapatra had told me. *Will I hit negative black swan if I leave this organisation?*

-x-

VIII

On the second day of my leave, I got a call from Vinay, who had done some serious research with the help of his friend in the tourism ministry.

"Varun, I could not find any temple where Crowns are offered to God. However, based on your dream and temple location, my friend was able to find four temples. I am sending you pics of all the four temples. Please check and confirm if any of these matches the temple you are searching for."

"Thanks a ton, dude! I'll check and confirm in the next few minutes." I ran towards my PC and opened my mailbox. I could see an email from Vinay in the mailbox. I opened the email and downloaded all the pics. Unfortunately, none of them matched the temple that I saw in my dreams.

I was disappointed. I immediately called up Vinay and told him the same.

Vinay was disappointed too and said in Hindi, "Ab Mukut waala Ishwar mandir Kahan milega?"

which translates into "Now where will we find the crown God temple?"

Something struck me suddenly. 'Mukut' means Crown and 'Ishwar' means God. If I join these two words, it becomes "MukutIshwar" resembling another word, "Mukteshwar" which is another name for Lord Shiva, which means God of eternal life. But the similarities were too great to be ignored.

"Vinay, I'll call you back in a few minutes." And I dropped the call.

The next thing I did was to search for "Mukteshwar" on the internet. The results were astonishing. I found two temples with the name 'Mukteshwar', one in Southern India and one in Northern India at the foot of Kumaon Mountain range near Nainital, a very popular hill station. The temple in Southern India was ruled out as there are no snow-clad mountains in the Southern part of India. So I focused more on the one closer to Nainital. The job was not done. I wanted to make sure that it is 'THE TEMPLE' and started searching over the internet for 'Mukteshwar Temple' and what I found sent chills over my spine. The same temple, the same stairs, the same valley, mountains and view from the temple backyard was in front of me.

I called Vinay immediately and said, "Dude, your Hindi made my day today. The temple which I was searching is in Mukteshwar and I got this clue from you when you said 'Mukut waala Ishwar'"

"Dude, Mukut and Mukt are different. 'Mukt' means 'getting released' while 'Mukut' means crown." Vinay was a perfectionist and was proud of his Hindi. He would not leave any opportunity to debate on language skills.

"It doesn't matter now. I found the temple I was searching for. I now understand what that falling into the valley means." I was thinking out loud, "The dream initially wanted to give me the clue of releasing from life and death when I fell into the valley, i.e. getting 'Mukt' but when I did not understand the clue, it gave me another clue, this time a language one 'Mukut' which is the crown and spelled very similar to 'Mukt'."

 "Great! So when are we going?" Asked Vinay

"Vinay, this time, I want to go there alone. I am planning a vacation with my family next week. I plan to take my family along to the nearby places but I will go alone to Mukteshwar"

"Dude, but…"

"No Vinay. This is decided."

"As you wish! But stay away from the valley. I want to see you return safely." Said a concerned Vinay who knew how stubborn I am.

-x-

Now, I wanted to tell to my wife but not to my parents or any other relatives. I did not want them to be worried about me.

That night, after our daughter had slept, I told the entire story about my dream, what happened in the US and how I was able to find the temple.

My wife, at first, did not believe me. Then, by sensing the intensity in my voice and eyes, she realised that it was indeed true. As always, she instantly agreed to accompany me. The only part that I didn't tell her was that I wanted to go to Mukteshwar alone. She would have never agreed to it. I didn't want to risk the life of my wife or my daughter; especially due to the dreadful ending of my dream and the fear instilled in me by people surrounding me.

While we were busy discussing my dream, we did not realise that my daughter was not fully asleep and heard our conversation.

The minute we concluded our discussion, she sprung up from her bed, which was just beside ours' and said, "Hurray Papa! We are going to see snow and we are going to a temple and your dream is coming true just like the princess story."

We had a tough time to tone down her excitement and at last, she slept when we narrated her story from her favourite princess book.

-x-

The next morning was equally action-packed. Apparently, my daughter had told my parents that we were planning a trip to 'Papa's dream temple'.

My parents were worried and curious at the same time. They wanted to know the details.

When I narrated all the incidents to them, my mom was especially very worried and adamant that I should not go there. She was sure that this has a relation to my previous lives. She started telling me stories about what had happened to a person somewhere in 'Rajasthan' when he discovered his past life through his dream and forgot his current life parents and wife.

"Where do you find such information, mom!", I asked her.

"They showed it on the news channel." She was on the verge of a breakdown, "Don't go there, Son. We have everything in life. Don't chase that dream for our sake."

All the emotional blackmailing had started.

-x-

It was customary of everyone in my cousin's immediate family to visit a Spiritual Guru after any major event like marriage, studies, having kids, etc. This time was no different. After the wedding last week, my cousin's family was going to the Guru's 'Ashram', which is the Hindi name for "the hermitage or the monarch". We had also accompanied them. My mother had her own agenda of presenting this problem of mine, where I was planning to go to a temple based on my dreams.

When they reached the 'Ashram', the couple first went and took the blessings. Then my mom went to the Guru and explained this problem to Him.

The Guru asked me to go closer to him and said, "Son, why don't you listen to your mother?"

"Sir, I am just curious."

"Curiosity! It is dangerous!", interrupted my mom. The Guru interrupted her and said that he will explain this to me in private.

The Guru could very well guess that my mom was emotional at that time and would not allow the discussion to go in the right direction either way.

I was guided to a cabin, probably a private meeting place in the 'Ashram'. I was asked to sit on the ground with folded legs in front of a 'throne-like' chair, which I assumed was for the Guru. The cabin was in all whites and silver. The guru, who also wore a white robe with silver border came in along with his two subordinates and sat on the chair.

The Guru ordered his subordinates to leave the room and not to be disturbed for the next few minutes. The subordinates obliged.

"Varun, you want to visit a place that you saw in your dream. Do you think it is safe?"

"Sir, with due respect, I don't think the place is unsafe. It is an ancient temple of Lord Shiva. Why do you think it is dangerous?"

"Varun, the temple itself may not be dangerous. But it is possible that some evil forces are inviting you to the place and have a plan to cause some harm before you enter the temple or after you move out of the temple. Don't you see that as a possibility?"

"Sir, I don't believe in evil forces. Even if such forces exist, why would they cause me any harm? What wrong have I done to them?"

"Don't underestimate the evil forces!" I could see a fire in Guru's eyes. "They can be made to cause harm to you by your enemies. I strongly advise you not to go to Mukteshwar"

"Sir, my mom is an ardent devotee of Lord Shiva. If I am visiting His temple, I am sure, He will not let anything happen to me"

"Son, don't be foolish. Think about it. I can only guide you but not stop you."

"Sir, I respect you. But I have to know my destiny." I offered 'Namaste' that is holding both palms perpendicular to the arm and parallel to the nose. This denotes offering respect. Then I left.

My mom was waiting outside for me and the moment I came out, she started asking me, "What did Guru say? You are not going right?"

I was again in a dilemma. Should I go there? Is it really safe? Does it have something to do with my past life? Is anyone doing black magic on me? Is it going to reveal anything about my destiny?

With these questions in my mind and my mom's fears, I thought it safe to postpone this discussion to another day. So I told my mom,

"Mom, I have not decided yet. I am thinking."

My mom was calm after hearing this, at least for now.

The dream continued to appear that night and the next night. That left me with no other options but to consult someone who could guide me. That someone, who had left a lasting impression on me, right after the first meeting! Mr. Mahapatra.

I saw the same dream, again!

-x-

IX

"Hello! Varun, Glad to hear your voice. How are you doing?", greeted Mr. Mahapatra. I had not called him up since our discussion on the flight close to a month ago. But today, I really felt that I need to speak to a person who can transfer some positivity into me. And the inflow of positivity had already started. My name is a very common name in India; still, Mr. Mahapatra instantly recognised me, just with my first name and voice. *He is very good with people. And more importantly, he still remembers me.* These thoughts in my mind delayed my response by a few seconds.

"Are you still there?", enquired Mr. Mahapatra

"Yes. Yes. I am. Sorry, I was lost in thoughts about our last discussion."

"Oh Yes. Do you still remember that?"

"Absolutely! In fact, I want to talk to you and understand more about your life." I was pretty fast to get to the point, as usual, without even asking how he was doing. I realised that and asked him, "Sir, By the way, how are you doing? How is your trip going on so far"?

"We are doing good. Everything is fine over here. We are returning next week."

"So soon this time! I thought you would be out for a few months at least."

"That's true. This time, someone needs us back home. My sister is going to be a grandmother soon. So she has to visit Australia to be with her daughter during her pregnancy and someone has to be home to take care of my ailing father", he sent a fake laugh to conclude this sentence. I could realise that he was stuck between his responsibility towards his parents and his desire to spend some more time with his children and grandchildren. He had chosen to tone down his desire and focus on his responsibility and was going through an internal fight, at least which is what I could grasp.

He sensed my silence and continued, "So, how are things at your end? You want to speak about something?"

I felt that it is better to meet Mr. Mahapatra personally since he will be back in a week. Hence I said, "I can wait till you are back"

"Drop by my place in Hyderabad. You have the address."

"Sure Sir. I'll call you after a few days" and we concluded the call.

-x-

It was around 8 am on a Saturday morning when Mr. Mahapatra had asked me to visit him at his residence. It was a rather unusual time for a weekend. But then I thought, for a retired person, all days are alike and thought that he had some plans during the day and hence wanted to speak to me before going out. I started from my home around 7:30 am although his residence was a ten-minute drive on a lazy Saturday morning. When I reached the main gate of his residence, it was still fifteen minutes to eight. I didn't want to disturb him before the allotted time. Hence, I thought of wandering in the colony. I drove my car slowly through the colony where he was living. Two things caught my attention. First was the fact that the colony was rather neatly planned with orthogonal streets and avenues, similarly built row houses, well-maintained park and a farm within the colony which had different vegetable and fruit plantation. The second thing was that none of the houses had any Digital TV antenna or the dish receptor.

Then I saw Mr. Mahapatra walking beside the farm towards his house. *He must have gone for a morning walk*. I thought. I went towards his house and parked my vehicle outside the gate and waited for him there.

When Mr. Mahapatra came closer to me, he recognised me and greeted with a warm smile. I responded similarly. As he was entering his gate, I could see that his shirt had dirt on it which I was staring at. He noticed me and told me that he is just back from the farm where he might have spilled some dirt on his shirt while weeding the bean saplings. I didn't know how to respond.

Why did he go to the farm in the first place?

I followed him into his drawing room with plenty of questions in my mind, in fact, more questions than what I had before I started from home this morning.

I sat in the drawing-room while he went inside to quickly change his clothes. While waiting for him, I observed that his drawing-room was suspiciously simple and neat. It had a set of wooden sofa which was maintained very well. There was a bookshelf towards one side of the room with a table and chair near it. A study light hung from the ceiling, sufficient enough to allow anyone sitting on the chair to read the books in ample light. A closed laptop – actually a MacBook was lying on the table. There was no Television in the room.

Before I could complete my review of the room, Mr. Mahapatra was back in the drawing-room with a cheerful smile on his face.

"Do you want to have coffee or tea?"

"Coffee, please." Aunt could hear us from the adjacent kitchen and she acknowledged, "In 2 minutes"

"So, how are things Varun?"

"Nothing new, Sir. They are as usual. How is your dad? How was your trip?"

"Dad is fine. He's still with my sister. He will be here tomorrow." He continued, "Trip was good. Always good to see children and grandchildren"

Aunt had brought coffee and kept it on a table. Uncle started preparing my coffee and enquired, "How many spoons of sugar?"

"One would do, Sir."

"So what do you want to talk about?", he asked while preparing coffee for me.

"Sir, I wanted your advice on something personal. I also had some questions regarding the way you handled your life between the age of twenty and sixty. But when I came here, I had a few more questions, which I feel are related to your lifestyle"

"Shoot them, Kid." After a pause, when he realised that I was having trouble asking about his present lifestyle, he himself continued, "Regarding my lifestyle now, it is vastly different from what it used to be in those forty years, I call them my forty years. Now I am leading a life of simplicity and health, very similar to what was the third stage of Ashram Dharma as per our ancient civilisation."

As per Ashram Dharma, every person's life is divided into four stages or Ashrams. The first stage is the Brahmacharya Ashram which indicates a stage of gaining knowledge. The second stage is the Grahasta Ashram, which comprises of a person fulfilling household duties in society as a Son, husband, and a father. The third stage is the Vanaprastha Ashram where the person starts living in a forestlike environment, slowly detaching himself from worldly desires. The fourth and final stage is the Sanyasa Ashram where the person is fully detached from worldly desires.

He continued, "I don't feel the need to go for the fourth stage of fully detaching myself from worldly desires. Hence, for me, there are only three stages in life – Learn, Live, Be Humble. Learn until you are 20-25 years of age. Live life to the fullest till sixty. There onwards, slowly reduce the worldly attachments and lead a simple humble life, probably the way that lets you meet your goals of a healthy happy life."

"So, is it the reason that you chose to live in this colony?"

He nodded slightly, "For me, this house has everything that a person of my age would need. It is centrally located, very close to all amenities. The colony is very calm and peaceful with everyone leading a simple life. There are close to fifty houses in the colony and everyone has to abide by the rules of the colony. Our day starts around 6 am with physical exercise which includes gardening, watering the lawns in the park and at the side of the roads, plucking fruits and vegetables and distributing among ourselves, etc. After our breakfast, for a few hours, we perform duties as per our expertise. People who were electricians take care of any minor electrical repairs, people like me who are interested to teach, teach in the nearby schools as part-time teachers. Retired civil engineers take care of road and house repairs and so on. We take rest after our lunch and meet in the evening as per our convenience and spend time socialising."

"Sir, how did you prepare yourself for such a simple life?"

"Son, the secret lies in those forty years. The better you manage those forty years, the more satisfied you will be after sixty. As I told you before, I never parked any of my dreams for post-retirement. I lived my life to the fullest, while not ignoring my duties as a Son, husband, and father. Anyone who lived his life to the fullest can detach himself from worldly pleasures easily."

"How were you able to do that? What is the secret formula? I am thirty-two now. More than ten years since I finished my education, i.e. the Learn stage as per your theory. I should ideally be in the 'Live' stage enjoying every bit of my life without compromising on the family. But here I am where I am not able to meet either of the goals. Neither I am able to live my life the way I would want to, nor am I able to secure a bright future for my family and the possibility of a tension-free life post-retirement."

"Son, the two goals that you mentioned are actually two facets of the same goal; that of being able to handle your life; being in total control of your life."

"Sir, that is a distant dream in the corporate world. With the kind of pressures that we have today, it is very difficult to be in control of one's life."

Mr. Mahapatra smiled. While he smiled, I could see a sense of sadness in his eyes as if someone reminded him of the worst nightmare.

I could not stop myself from saying, "Sorry sir! I didn't mean to hurt you. I am sure every generation has different kinds of challenges and in no means was I attempting to convey that life in your time was easier."

Mr. Mahapatra sighed and nodded. He got up from his seat, went towards his bookshelf and pulled out an old picture from one of the books. He kept on staring at the picture in grief while returning to his chair and after sitting down, he showed me the picture.

The picture had a middle-aged person, probably in his forties, seated on a chair with a teenager standing to his left and a six-seven-year-old boy to his right. Another baby was in his lap.

"That's me!" said Mr. Mahapatra pointing towards the young boy.

"Is that your father, Sir?" I asked.

"Yes. And the one on his lap is my sister. The teenager standing to my father's right was my elder brother. My best friend!", He continued, "My mother died soon after my sister was born. When my father was busy with his job, trying to make ends meet, my grandmother would take care of my sister. It was my brother who would give me the parental love that I deserved at a tender age of six."

"I see. Where is he now?", I was still trying to understand what made Mr. Mahapatra sad.

"I killed him." And he broke down into tears. Mrs. Mahapatra was quick to react. She was out there in a flash with a glass of water and the asthma spray to contain a possible attack, which could have occurred due to the sudden burst of emotion.

I was all shocked and clueless about how to behave. I had only seen a strong Mahapatra so far and to see a role model in such a state was making me feel guilty. I kept on repeating, "Sir, are you ok? Should I call the doctor?"

It took a few minutes before Mr. Mahapatra settled down. As he was back to his normal self, I thought of leaving for the day with the guilt of having caused enough pain to the aged person. As I was about to stand, Mr. Mahapatra signalled with his hand to sit down and continued, "Son, it is not your fault. My life will pass haunted by this remorse. My brother was very studious and my father had this only dream of seeing him as the district collector. But my brother was tired of the poverty that we were seeing and was keen on helping my father in earning money. So, while he was still doing undergraduation, he joined a part-time job in a coaching institute without my father's permission and started making some money. One day, suddenly, someone came to my father telling him that my brother had done something wrong and the crowd was hitting him. I was too young to ask him what had happened but all I remember is that my brother came home bleeding that day and my dad was very upset. There was a heated argument between my dad and my brother that night followed by my father leaving the house. After my father left the house, I went to my brother and asked him if the wounds are hurting.

He replied, "Not anymore, my brother! He looked into my eyes and asked me if I trusted him."

I replied in affirmative.

He continued, "I will never do anything that would bring disrespect to our family. But the father does not seem to believe me." He was looking very disappointed and tired. He got up with great difficulty and was not in a position to walk. He asked me to go to the well and bring some water for him. I instantly went to the well, drew some water using the bucket that was suspended to a rope, and brought water for my brother in the same bucket as I could not find another tumbler nearby. He drank some water and asked me to sleep. I went to sleep only to be woken up by screams of my dad and grandmother. The sight of my brother hanging from the ceiling fan with the same rope that I had brought is still crystal clear to me. He could not bear the situation any longer and committed suicide. I am still not sure if he had decided to commit suicide before seeing the rope tied to the tumbler or only after I brought it."

Mr. Mahapatra almost choked while speaking the last few words. But he continued, "The next few months were very different for me. I saw my grandmother die, my father, getting paralysed. I had suddenly become the eldest fit member of the family even before I turned eight! None of the relatives, near or distant, ever paid any visit to our home. Even today, I don't know if I have any relatives alive. For the next three years, I did not go to school. I used to go to the bus stand and polish shoes for a tenth of a rupee and would earn just enough to eat a one-time meal for me, my sister and my father. I could see tears in my father's eyes as I fed him, possibly due to the guilt or helplessness or both. Then one day, someone informed us that we had owned some land in some village which can be sold to make some money, which we did. That improved the situation a bit for the next few years and I could at least appear for high school examinations via a part-time curriculum. After passing my high school examination, I was lucky enough to get a job in Railways as a class IV employee. I used to carry coal from the yard to the engine. I had the passion to do something, possibly due to the love of my brother, so I continued my part-time studies and appeared in intermediate examinations following which, I completed my Bachelor of Science in Physics. I was also smart enough to rise in ranks in Railways and had become an office administrator by the time I finished my graduation. Slowly and steadily, I was able to take care of my responsibilities by getting my sister married, giving medical attention to my father and so on. As I continued my part-time studies, I got better opportunities and eventually settled in the United States and now here I am. But the guilt remains. Whatever I do, I can never get rid of it."

I was stunned. It was an epiphany of sorts, on how lucky I was to never have to face such a situation in my life. I remained silent, not sure how to reinstate the conversation. Finally, I said, "Sorry Sir. I am extremely sorry. I was deeply involved in my own self when I spoke to you in such a harsh tone regarding my problems."

"Son, you need not be sorry. Our own problems always look big as we see them through magnifying glasses. If a hen starts thinking what will happen to its egg- whether it will hatch or not, whether someone will kill the chicken or eat as egg, it will not be able to enjoy even the few moments the chicken is alive. We should always look at our problems from someone else's eyes and try to solve our problems as if they are not ours but someone else's."

I had many more questions for him. In fact, the more important ones! But I felt that I should discuss those some other day and left for the day. While leaving, Mr. Mahapatra apologised for the emotional outburst and asked me to visit him the next day same time to continue the discussion as he was aware that I still had unanswered queries.

-x-

The next day, I went to his home slightly early, parked my car outside his house and went to the farm where he spent his mornings daily.

He saw me from a distance and waved at me, showing me the walkway which could be used to reach him without harming the plantation.

When I went closer, he said, "Welcome, Son! I knew you will be early today. Come, let's weed out the bean saplings."

I took a shovel and started weeding out under his supervision. Once I had understood the way to separate out weed from the sapling, Mr. Mahapatra said in a joyous tone, "See, this is all we need to learn to do. Separate out the weed from plants." He was obviously using a metaphor of weed for the problems and plants for life. I understood what he was trying to indicate and started asking my questions.

"Sir, yesterday, you mentioned about looking at your problems as if they are someone else's. Is this how you were able to live those forty years happily without any regret?"

"That's not it, Son", He paused his work for a few seconds, bent his head at an angle that would make him easy to look straight into my eyes through his glasses and said, "You should learn to identify options that you have at every stage of your life. Once you identify those, you should weigh the options keeping your dreams and responsibilities in mind and choose the option that would help you in the right direction towards your goal."

"That's it?"

"Son, it is easier said than done. If you are choosing your options, you are also rejecting other options. And to reject an option, you should know how to say 'No'. That is the most difficult thing to do for a sincere person."

I was silently listening. I could correlate the words with what had happened in the office. I was doing what I was being told to do. I was not even looking for other options. At that moment, I could think of numerous situations where I had some other option, but I chose to ignore those.

Mr. Mahapatra also allowed me to absorb this concept of 'being in control of one's life'. So he waited for me to speak up. For the next twenty-odd minutes, the two of us were silent; I was deeply involved in my thoughts while my hands were involuntarily weeding the plants. This deadlock was interrupted when it was time to go home.

Even on the short walk to his home, we were silent. We went inside his house, washed our hands and feet and sat on the sofa. Mrs. Mahapatra had served breakfast for the two of us. For the next few minutes, I had to concentrate on our breakfast plates as Mrs. Mahapatra would replenish our plates with more food. Finally, I had to set my plate aside to stop that.

After our breakfast, Mr. Mahapatra asked me, "What are you searching for? What are your thoughts? What do you want to do and achieve? These are very difficult questions to answer. Sometimes, one's lifetime is not sufficient to find answers to these questions. So replace those with short term planning with the possible options in front of you. Live life in the present with near-future vision! For example, don't focus on what you want to do after retirement or what you want to do before retirement or when you want to retire. Instead, focus on what you want to do in the next six months."

While he was speaking these words, of all the things that were going in my mind, the first thing that came in my mind was that I have an option here, either I can visit Mukteshwar temple and clarify my doubts and superstitions about my destiny and its relation with the temple and dream or choose to not visit the temple and carry the burden on myself for the rest of the life. The second option appeared to me like trying to save myself from hitting negative black swan as told by Mr. Mahapatra during our first encounter at my first meeting in the flight. The first option was more logical as nothing wrong could happen scientifically and if something good is going to happen, I could hit the positive black swan! After all, I was in my 'own forty years'!

I had learned to identify the options at the current junction of my life and had also made a choice. It was all about walking through the chosen path!

-x-

X

Once I had made my decision on going to Muk-teshwar, it was now important to do so, without hurting anyone; especially my mom. Also, I wanted to update Pallav regarding my findings; although I knew, it wouldn't be easy, keeping in mind, the last communication we had, in this regard. Pallav had insisted that I stop chasing my dream since he had seen a lot of people lose everything, trying to do so.

The first step was to build a story that is believable. I had to use the story, not just to hide the fact that I was going to visit Mukteshwar, but also my inten-tion to visit it alone. What this would mean is that my wife also needs to believe in it.

That night, after dinner, I told my wife that there is something that I wanted to tell her. She sensed that it was regarding my dream and signalled me to hold on for a while. The next moment, I realised the reason she did so. Karishma slowly checked the blanket of my daughter, confirmed that her eyes were closed and said in a soft but audible tone,

"Let's have ice cream now! Pinky is asleep." And she waited for a response from our daughter. There wasn't any! This was her way of confirming that my daughter is actually asleep.

Karishma turned towards me and said, "Now tell me, honey! I didn't want the scene from the last time to repeat. Hence just double confirming if Pinky is asleep."

"That's fine. So, what I was saying was that we should visit Mukteshwar. Unless we do so, I don't think, I will find my… I mean our destiny." I stumbled with my words as I had never lied to my family so far. I might have hidden a few facts, here and there, but never lied. I had an extremely friendly relationship with Karishma, which never needed any lie.

"What will you tell Mom?" was the immediate response from Karishma. We already had this discussion on why this trip was important for me and Karishma appreciated every bit of it and as usual, was supporting me.

"Do you remember Rahul Singh? The tall guy in school, who joined the National Defence Academy."

"Yes. I do. He was a few years senior to us, I believe."

"Hmm. He is on my friends' list on Facebook and is currently posted at Ranikhet, which is very close to Mukteshwar. I have connected with him and he is willing to arrange for a Lecture in their regiment which I will have to deliver."

"What lecture will you deliver to the Indian Army?" asked Karishma in a teasing mode.

"Well. I could give a full-day lecture on 'Miseries of Software Engineer' which could give them some sense of job satisfaction" I joked back which was not well taken by Karishma. Karishma had high regard for the Indian Army. She would get irritated whenever some jokes are named after them. Even I respect Indian Army for the sacrifices they make for us, but this joke was more of a slip of my tongue, which I immediately realised and apologised.

"Sorry. I didn't mean to hurt you. It was just a bad joke. In fact, Rahul told me that their regiment is planning to request for new software to analyse the movements across the border. He wanted me to deliver a lecture on how requirements are documented."

"That's cool. Can I be part of that lecture too?" asked an enthusiastic Karishma.

"I can't guarantee that. Let me check with Rahul."

"Ok... so you are going to tell everyone that we are going to Ranikhet to attend a seminar."

"Mom does not know that Ranikhet and Mukteshwar are close by. She only knows that Mukteshwar is near Nainital." When I said this, I was not very confident if my mom would know this. But I took a chance.

"Sounds like a plan. But keep the same story for Pinky and the rest of the family members too. We don't want to maintain different versions."

I nodded.

"Accha chalo, we need to sleep now. It is already late and tomorrow is going to be a long day. We also have Pinky's Parent-Teacher meeting. Good Night"

"Good Night, Karishma!" I sighed a relief wanting a pat on my back to have managed my first lie to my wife. You got it right! The entire story of Rahul was cooked up. I wanted to go to Mukteshwar alone by leaving Karishma and Pinky at the hotel, with the pretext of going to the seminar. Karishma was otherwise adamant to accompany me to Mukteshwar. *How can I risk the lives of my family for my madness?*

The next morning, it was Karishma's job to inform my mom, casually, about my seminar at the Indian Army regiment. She and my mom were in the kitchen, and Karishma found the right opportunity.

"Mom! Pinky has holidays from tomorrow. We need not get up so early. So good naa?" Karishma said, to initiate a dialogue.

"Hmm… at least the poor kid will get some rest." My mom always had this soft corner for Pinky as she had to leave for school at 6:30 am in the morning.

"Right. In fact, it has been a while since we took her out. It seems Varun has some office seminar with the Indian Army at a hill station. I was thinking that we all should accompany him." Karishma knew that my mom and dad will not accompany us as they don't like traveling a lot.

"No dear! Your Father-in-law would not want to travel. We are happy here. Why don't you guys accompany Varun?" The dialogue had started to give results in the direction of our script, but before Karishma could start celebrating, mom asked back, "Where is this seminar?"

"Ranikhet, mom", said Karishma

"Ranikhet! It should be the Kumaon regiment! My cousin, Mahendra is in Almora. Ranikhet is in the Almora district in Uttarakhand. He is a government official in the Electricity Department of Almora. Mahendra has been inviting us to visit him for a long time. You guys should visit him…." Mom stopped for a while, thinking about something and said, "Karishma, if you guys are going to Ranikhet, just be careful, Mukteshwar should be nearby. Don't let Varun know this. Else this will trigger his thought to visit that doomed temple again!"

These last few statements were a shocker for Karishma. We had underestimated my mother's knowledge. Karishma stammered but gathered her senses and said, "Is it? Sure, Mom!"

My mom sensed something on her face and started cross-questioning her, "So is Varun going for this assignment via his office?"

"Yes, mom. It seems his company is building some software for the Indian Army."

"How long will be the trip?"

"Should be for a few days, plus a few additional days for vacation." These questions were starting to trouble Karishma as the story was changing now.

"Good. Remember. No Mukteshwar! I will ask Mahendra to arrange for your accommodation."

"No Mukteshwar. Promise mom. I wouldn't even tell Varun. Accommodation will be arranged by the office. So no need to trouble Mahendra Uncle"

"Arey… That's no trouble for him. He would be more than happy to see you guys. Let me speak to him immediately." Mom picked up her phone and dialed a number and went to her bedroom to speak to her cousin in private. Karishma had started to panic. She rushed to me and narrated the entire story to me.

"So far, so good." Was my instant response "I didn't expect mom to buy our story so easily!"

"You think so? Mom is arranging a shadow for us, in the form of her cousin Mahendra. We better be careful" cautioned Karishma.

"Don't worry! We will manage that."

Mom had finished talking to Mahendra Uncle and was looking for us. She caught hold of me once I went to the drawing-room.

"Varun, Karishma told me that you are going for some seminar at Ranikhet. Your uncle, Mahendra stays close by. He will arrange for everything you need there."

"Thanks, mom. But that may not be needed. There will be others from the office and we all will be staying at the Army guest house in Ranikhet. We will meet him for sure."

"Varun, your uncle will feel bad if you don't stay with him"

"Mom! I am going on an official visit. Once my official visit is done, we will stay with him. Don't trouble me." I was slightly harsh on my response which hurt my mom.

"I am always trouble for you."

"Sorry, mom. Please understand. I have to stay with my colleagues. Else trip would not be successful."

"Ok. But take care. And listen to Karishma. Don't go anywhere alone."

"I promise." Another lie and another false promise! But I was helpless.

With this recent development, I had to change my plan a bit. First, I had to prepare a dummy exclusive pass for the Army Cantonment area for which I designed a pass and got it printed on matte paper to give a real feel to it.

Second, I had earlier thought of leaving Karishma and Pinky at the hotel while I visit Mukteshwar. But now, I had a better plan of leaving them at Uncle Mahendra's place. That way, if something happens to me at Mukteshwar, Uncle Mahendra can take care of their safety.

The plan was perfect. At least on paper!

Once this mission of storytelling to Karishma and mom was accomplished, I had to move to the second item on my agenda. That of informing Pallav! I wanted to be extremely careful here, so as to not hurt anyone. This is what I wrote to Pallav

"Dear Pallav,

How are you doing? You have really been of great help in deciphering my dream. But there is some recent development to my dream. I found the exact temple. I never visited this place but saw it in my dreams.

I respect your advice to stop chasing my dream and I really stopped chasing it, until I discovered the temple.

Now that I know where the temple is, it is getting difficult for me, to forget the dream. Trying to forget the dream has become more painful than chasing the dream. Hence I am taking this decision to visit the temple and close this chapter once and for all.

I know, it is not exactly, what you wanted me to do, but there could be no other way for me to get out of this mess.

I hope you understand.

Warm Regards,

Varun"

I did not get any response to this email. I had assumed that Pallav is unhappy with my decision and is hence avoiding me. But I didn't have a choice.

I had planned to travel in three days. I booked our flight tickets to Delhi, booked a cab from Delhi for four days to stay with us for the entire trip and also booked a room in a resort in Ranikhet.

I tried searching for the hotel which resembled the one from my dream but failed to find one. Hence, I booked the resort which had the best reviews within the budget that we had. The resort that I booked also boasted of having a panoramic view of the mighty Himalayan Mountain range, which I had seen in my dream.

My daughter, Pinky, who was five years old, was all excited and gave her suggestions on what she wants to do, how the hotel should be and so on.

Karishma and Pinky were busy shopping for most of the next two days, while I was doing my 'Ph.D.' researching the GPS signal, cellphone signals, 3G coverage, etc. Wherever I felt that there wouldn't be any signals, I had taken snapshots of the zoomed maps and stored on my mobile.

As I was taking my family on a trip after a long gap, I wanted to make it a memorable one and hence, had to create a fun-filled itinerary for them. Also, I wanted to make this a light trip, to avoid overthinking about Mukteshwar or my dream which could cause anxiety.

-x-

XI

On the day of the journey, as we were taking a cab to the airport, I saw my mom talking to Karishma in private. I could also see the worry in my mom's eyes. On our way to the airport, Karishma told me that my mom had reiterated the fact that I should not visit Mukteshwar. She was very innocent and we were cheating her by telling lies. I had to convince Karishma that we were not cheating her, but just making her feel comfortable while we are away.

We checked-in our luggage and boarded the flight. The flight took off on time and reached Delhi airport on time. The economy flight did not even have proper meals on board. Hence we were hungry when we came out of the arrivals gate. We had to locate the cab driver first.

To our pleasure, we could see a tall guy dressed in white & white, without a cap holding a placard with 'Mr. & Mrs. Varun' printed on it. We contacted him, dumped all our luggage in his cab and asked for a good restaurant nearby. The driver, Fateh Mohammed, gave us specific options – if we want south Indian, there was a good restaurant in the airport itself. For north Indian, he told that we could visit Haldirams. We opted for Haldirams, which was on the way to Ranikhet. We had a nice meal and continued our journey with a stomach full of food and eyes full of sleep!

We had slept for an hour or maybe more, only to be woken up by Mohammed, asking if we would want to have tea. We got down from the cab, had a nice cup of traditional tea. Pinky wanted to have mango juice which we found at the nearby shop.

When we resumed our journey after the short break, I was feeling fresh. I started having a casual chat with Mohammed on where he was from, and how long he has been driving, etc. As we discussed varied things, we crossed a very wide river. Mohammed stopped the cab for a while and offered his respect to the river, took some water and drank it. He also brought some water from the river and said,

"Sir, this is sacred water of the Holy Ganges!" and he poured some water in our hands. We reluctantly took a sip and poured the rest on our heads, in a gesture of respect to the river. This was me seeing the Ganges, the holy river often referred to as

Mother Ganga. The sheer width and volume of water were enough to bring a sense of respect to everyone.

When Mohammed started the cab, I asked him, "Do you also respect the Ganges?" my question was, of course, related to his name, which is a Muslim name and Ganges is a sacred river often personified as a deity for the Hindus.

"Yes, Sir. People from my religion do not refer to the Ganges as a Goddess but I have immense respect for the river. During my ten years as a driver, I have seen numerous people, mostly Hindus, craving to have a single glimpse of this river in their lifetime. They are even willing to wait at the bank of this very river until the end of their life. Such stories have inspired me a lot and I feel that it is special. I don't know in what sense, but I feel blessed every time I touch the waters of this river. Even if the water looks murky, drinking it never caused me any harm. Call it faith or something else; I just like the Ganges."

That response changed my perception of religion. It is we, who divide the natural resources as belonging to a religion, region, caste, etc. But once we uncover ourselves and look deep inside, the resources belong equally to all the people. The fact that a river, which I had heard as holy and never experienced it myself, could have such a beautiful impact on a person, just based on belief, touched me to the core and I myself could see the beauty of the river Ganges.

It was at that moment, that I realised that this trip is not going to be a usual one for me. It is going to be an experience in itself which I was eagerly waiting for!

Our next stop was at Rampur, which was famous for hand-made knives. After a snack break, we walked around the knife market, only to be astonished by the wide range of knives ranging from a pocket foldable knife to a butcher's knife. While I was reluctant to buy one, Karishma bought a foldable knife. This purchase found its utility within the next thirty minutes. On our onward journey, for a stretch of three to four kilometres, on either side of the road, we could see huge privately owned orchids of guava and peaches. Pinky on the rear seat was jumping up and down with joy of seeing so many trees full of fruits. We stopped at one of the orchids, went inside and plucked guavas and peaches. The guavas were the largest, that I have ever seen in my life, almost of the size of a baseball. Pinky plucked a few fruits too!

The fruits were so big that, we had to inaugurate the newly purchased knife of the proud owner, Karishma, whose face was showing intelligence, elegance, and majesty at the same time for her decision to purchase the knife, however small it may be. As Karishma cut the fruits into quarters, Mohammed warned us about the possibility of worms inside. To our disgust, we found some seed coloured worms inside the fully ripened guava, which scared Pinky away. Pinky vowed to never touch ripened guavas again. Back in Hyderabad, the guavas are not that big, but we never saw worms! Or maybe we just never saw those.

Mohammed informed us that we should resume traveling so that we reach Ranikhet before sunset. The road beyond Haldwani was a curvy one with sharp curves and it was safe to reach while the sun was shining. We got into the cab and proceeded for Ranikhet. The route was not as bad as I had thought, based on my past experience with curvy roads in the United States, especially the one that led to Sequoia National Park in California.

It was around 7 pm by the time we reached Ranikhet. We checked into the hotel. This hotel reception or the elevation was nowhere close to what I had seen in my dream but didn't I know that while booking? I was just too ambitiously hoping that it is the same hotel. Before I went to my room, I confirmed with the staff regarding the arrangements for our driver, Mohammed. The staff showed me a large dormitory with blankets, pillows, and lockers for the drivers. This was satisfactory. Karishma and Pinky had already reached the room and were exploring the surroundings. I joined them in the room. The room was again not what I had seen in the dream, but the sit out looked similar. I went and stood in the sit out for some time, as long as I could bear the cold and see the dark blue borders of the mountain ranges and lights of the buildings visible. We had a traditional vegetarian Kumaon dinner that night which included potato curry and bread made of unknown flour. The hotel had also arranged for a campfire for residents and we had a nice little time around the fire, which reminded us of our school picnics and industry visits.

-x-

I saw the same dream, again!

XII

I had told Karishma that we will visit Mukteshwar on the third day of our trip after 'my fake seminar' was complete. I had made up my mind to visit Mukteshwar on the second day alone. Hence I had created a three-day itinerary to cover the surrounding areas. On the first day, we were to visit local Ranikhet and make a scenic trip to Kausani. The second day, we were to visit Almora. I had told Karishma that I will drop her and Pinky at Uncle Mahendra's place before proceeding for the seminar. I had also informed her that her visit to the Cantonment for the seminar was not approved by the Indian Army due to the presence of a child. She bought that idea easily, based on my face value. As per my itinerary, we were to visit Mukteshwar early in the morning on the third day, before going to Nainital.

Day one, we woke up slightly late. It was all foggy and all our attempts, to catch a glimpse of the Mighty Himalayas, proved futile. The restaurant had a picture of the Himalayan view and the waiter gave us a virtual tour of the Himalayas showing the picture. After we were done with the complimentary breakfast, we headed to the front desk where Mohammed was waiting, all set to take us to Kausani.

While Kausani was just a village, some sixty kilometres away, the route from Ranikhet to Kausani was very scenic with the picturesque landscape all through. There was a stream beside the curvy road throughout the journey. The flowing water from the stream made a pleasant virgin gushing sound as it found its way downstream. We came across more than twenty metal foot-bridges over the stream, which were used by villagers to walk from one hill to the other, separated by this stream. We stopped at numerous places and took snaps. Mohammed doubled up as a photographer for us! At one viewpoint, we could see a lone house, with a windmill in the background, in the middle of tens of hectares of greenery with the stream dividing the farm as if it were two pieces of a jigsaw puzzle, only to be again connected by the metal foot over bridge. I and Karishma were lost in ourselves for a good six minutes until we realised that we were not in Switzerland but in India, only after we saw something written in Hindi on the walls of the house.

Once we reached there around noon, what we saw at Kausani was nothing different from what we have anywhere else. Just a marketplace, few hotels, and restaurants! It was the journey that managed to bring a few smiles and wow moments and not the destination. Maybe we should compare our lives to this journey and think about enjoying the short milestones and journey as it happens instead of waiting for the destination!!

We had lunch at the marketplace and started the return journey using a different route, which crossed through the plains in the valley between Kausani and Ranikhet. The route was straight and took lesser time to cover, but was, again, very beautiful.

Pinky was too tired and she fell asleep on the way back and we had to carry her to the room once we reached the hotel in the evening. After getting refreshed, I spoke to uncle Mahendra and informed him that we will visit him the next day. We deliberately did not inform him about the seminar as I was worried that he may want to accompany me, thereby spoiling my plans to visit Mukteshwar alone.

We were very tired of continuous travel and slept before 9 pm, immediately after dinner. The next day was going to be a big day for me and I was excited as well as nervous for the same. I needed a night of sound sleep. I took some anti-anxiety pills, prescribed by my doctor, only to be taken on rare occasions and slept.

-X-

XIII

It was an extremely cold morning when I got up from my bed in the hotel and went to the sit-out to see the Sunrise. I could see nothing but darkness which was slowly fading away into a lighter self as the clock was ticking. The first thing I could notice was the heavy fog in the quiescent valley followed by a panoramic dark border of the mountain range beyond the valley. I could see the fog, (or were those clouds?) rise slowly as the border lightened, threatening to block the view of the mighty Himalayan range at the time of Sunrise. The arrival of the Sun to this part of the earth was proudly announced by Mount Trishul, which turned itself into golden white, even before the Sun was visible. It started turning white for the first time, but, not before cascading the golden colour to Mount Mrigathuni and Nandadevi. As I concentrated on the skyline of the Himalayas, some of the shapes that appeared as clouds so far, started to expose themselves as other peaks in the Himalayan range. It was an experience that made me forget everything else in life for a few seconds.

While I was deeply immersed in my newly found love in the Himalayas, with my hands holding the patio grill, I felt a pair of little warm hands holding my leg in excitement. My daughter was awake and was holding me firmly, probably due to the cold or fear of height or the marvellous sight of snow-clad mountains that she could see in front of her. As I was about to hold my daughter in front of me, with an attempt to explain to her the beauty of Himalayas, my wife joined us in the patio with a curious question, "Varun, does this view look familiar?"

She was indirectly asking me if the view was similar to the one in my dream. I nodded.

I could see a confused expression on Karishma's face. It was probably a mix of concern, surprise and excitement all at the same time. Before I could say anything, she changed the topic, "When do we have to leave for your uncle's place?"

"My seminar is at 11. I think, if we start by 7:30, we should be good." I wanted to be in the temple by 11; hence told the same time for the Seminar. As per my estimation, Mukteshwar was around an hour away from my uncle's place.

We quickly got ready, had our breakfast and went to the reception area, where we found the ever-

121

smiling Mohammed ready and waiting for us. We boarded the cab and started for Almora, the town where my uncle lived.

During the trip, I opted to sit on the rear seat with my family as I was feeling nervous, which was unusual in my nature. I would try not to leave the front seat empty as I felt it as a gesture of disrespect to the driver. This act of mine did not go unnoticed. Karishma's eyeball zoomed in and followed my eyes for a few seconds, while I was deliberately trying to avoid eye contact. Something was wrong with me at that time, perhaps due to my complex thoughts that were in the Brownian movement.

"Varun, are you ok?"

"Yes… yes… of course!" was my instant reply, "just trying to walk through my seminar in my mind". I got the right justification on time.

It took close to fifty minutes for us to reach my uncle's place. He was standing at the outer gate of his house while constantly on phone with me, giving directions. As we alighted, he gave me a fatherly pat with a side hug as if he is proud of me. It was his way of showing the happiness to see us. I had last seen Uncle Mahendra more than a few years ago. He was a distant cousin of my mom but was very close to my mom's family during their childhood.

I had some time based on my calculations. Hence I accompanied my family inside his house. After having a cup of coffee, I informed him that I have to go to the cantonment for a seminar. That started a stream of questions to me on where I was going, whom I was meeting and what is the seminar about. My uncle even offered to attend the seminar as he had that permanent VIP pass for the cantonment. But I told him that it is actually a private seminar cum workshop which has the agenda of some software related work at the Indian Army and it would be embarrassing for me to take someone else along in front of my boss. I am sure, I was a bit harsh, but I didn't have an option. Any slight leniency would have resulted in my plan going down the drains!

With this, I told my uncle, not to wait for me for lunch as it may get late and departed from there. I sat on the front seat in the cab and turned back to see my wife and daughter wave at me.

As we came out of the gated colony in which my uncle resided, I told Mohammed of my plan to visit Mukteshwar. He was slightly surprised but didn't say anything. I told him not to tell anything to my wife if she calls mid-way.

The route to Mukteshwar from Almora was very beautiful with numerous apple orchids en-route. It took us a little more than an hour to reach Mukteshwar, thankfully due to the absence of fog. As we reached Mukteshwar town, my heartbeat started rising. I closed my eyes to find peace but peace was nowhere near me. I opened my eyes when Mohammed stopped the car and said, "Sir, we are at Mukteshwar Temple."

For a few seconds, I did not want to open my eyes and wanted to ask Mohammed to turn back. But I gathered all my guts to open my eyes and get out of the car. As I stepped out, I could sense suspiciously silent surroundings, so silent that I could hear the breeze gushing between the trees. As I stood there, I turned towards the sky, breathed a deep one and inspected the area in one shot. In one direction, I could see a familiar visual. There was an oval white arch at the foot of one of the hills. It was exactly the same, which I had seen in my dream. Now I could read what was written on the arch – It read, 'Mukteshwar Dham', which translates to the Abode of Mukteshwar.

I was feeling as if my feet are twice as heavy as normal, due to the involuntary reluctance to venture into the unknown, but I had made up my mind. I took slow steps towards the arch and slowly started climbing the staggered steps. I was frequently inspecting the surroundings in anticipation of any unknown dangers waiting my way.

When I climbed the stairs, it was again confirmed that I had dreamt of this exact place. I could see the exact same flat stoned surface, the asbestos shade, and the adjoining steps. I carefully inspected the area where I had dreamt of the devotees offering crowns to the deity. At the exact place, was a fireplace which was not lit at that time, but had the required setting to perform the offering ceremony as I dreamt of.

I walked further, took the steps and went to the main temple. As I stood in front of Lord Shiva's idol, a priest offered prayers to the Lord on my behalf. I took the blessings of the priest and started wandering in the temple, aimlessly. I didn't know what I was trying to decode. I found everything absolutely normal. But the temple did not give me a feeling of visiting a new place. I knew the whereabouts of the temple and could easily go to the temple backyard. On reaching the backyard, I could see a park nearby. But I decided against going to the park. I also saw the slanting rock and the beautiful Himalayan view behind it, looking exactly the way it was earlier that morning. I was tired and sat on the rock for a while.

While I was sitting on the rock, watching the view, my mind was time traveling. It seems it was after quite a time that I sat alone for so long without any purpose or distractions and my mind was optimally utilising the opportunity. I literally walked my life in those forty-odd minutes with all my life moments happening right in front of me. The thing that really baffled me was that the most emotional moments in my life were not the real milestones in my life. I hardly felt any emotions when I saw a younger myself getting a Gold Medal for State Rank in my intermediate. Ditto when I got placed into an MNC with a fat package or when I married my girlfriend or when my daughter was born. There was absolutely no flow of emotions.

What really brought an emotional flow of current were the minor moments in my life like the visual of my school, the day when I tripped my lunchbox and my friend shared his food with me in primary school, the day when I prepared hard for my cricket selection but ended up not going there, the numerous days when I practiced by knocking and bouncing the ball against the wall, the visual of me celebrating 'Diwali' in the town where I spent eighteen years of my life, the visuals of our under-construction house where I used to play in the sand after my school, our kitchen where I would sit on the counter top while my mom would make and serve hot Indian pancakes, one particular incident when I woke up at night and asked my mom to make sweet bread and she obliged without a hint of pain or hesitation, my dad who would take me around the town on his motorbike on the festive eves to show me the decorations and celebrations, me and my father playing badminton together, my father making and flying kites with me, my ride to school with friends with cricket bat hung to the carrier, the games period, the games that we played during the lunch break, the fallen tree in my college which witnessed numerous examination preparations, the wackiest professor who would not respond to questions if he felt that they were not good enough, the day I realised that my childhood friend, Karishma was the love of my life, numerous bunked classes for having cold coffee at a famous joint near my college, the day I proposed her, the Coonoor resort that we visited together, the Christmas celebrations in London, our rented house in London where we started our married life, the play area and the shopping centre near the house, our shopping together for our new house, the moment when my wife told me that she is pregnant, the day she wanted to eat something specific at an Indian restaurant during her second trimester, the moment I took my daughter in my hands for the first time forcefully as I was scared that I would trip her down.

It was getting very difficult for me to come out of the emotional turmoil when something happened which happened each and every time in my dream, some kind of distraction followed by push. This time, it was just a distraction to start with when my mobile phone rang. It was already noon and my wife had called me to check where I was, since everyone was waiting for me for lunch. I requested them to proceed with lunch as the relative's house was close to an hour's drive from the temple.

When I disconnected the call, I suddenly started feeling uneasy, not just because of the emotional journey that I went through but also because of the fright of some accident as it would happen in my dream. Hence I got up from the rock and started going out of the temple. I had to follow the same route via the main temple to descend the stairs.

When I crossed the main temple dome, I realised that nothing unusual had happened and I was not sure if I wanted something unusual to happen or not. As I was about to descend the first set of stairs, I heard a voice,

"Son, I know you have come very far to see this temple."

I turned around to find a very old sage sitting on the floor right on a small platform. The sage had long hair which was let loose on his face covering his face fully. He wore a small robe on his waist and had a wooden 'T' structure on which he had rested his hand.

While I was still unsure of who he was, he called me towards him and said, "Do you want to know a Secret?"

I was scared. For a moment, I felt that I didn't want to know anything about this temple or the association that I have with it.

What if I come to know about my past life?

But is that not why I traveled so far?

Do I believe in a past life or black magic as mom would think it is? Does it really matter if I believe in a past life or not?

Am I willing to listen to something that might change my life forever and further complicate it?

Am I willing to carry this burden of not knowing the reason for this dream for the entire life?

The only answer that I had for all these questions is that I am still not ready for this. I did not want to further complicate my life. If I have to learn about this dream, I should first be able to control my present life and do what I want to do.

At that point, the only thing I wanted to do was to go back and collect as many small moments as possible with my family, friends, and life. The forty minutes spent alone on the rock had changed my thinking.

I did not even have the courtesy to say something and escape from the temple. Instead, I started running, running really hard towards the stairs, got down the stairs and immediately sat in the taxi. I instructed the driver to drive to my uncle's home.

I was actually feeling better. It was a promise that I had made to myself that I will visit this temple again; not to uncover the mysteries but to relax and if I find anything at that time, I will not shy away from the same. But I will visit the temple only when I have good control over my life, the 'Maha-patra way'!

-x-

The driver took just about fifty minutes to reach my relative's home. When I reached there, as expected, they were still waiting for me to join them for lunch. I apologised for being late, got freshened up and went to the table for lunch. We spent a few hours together after lunch and then went back to Ranikhet.

At Ranikhet, we went to the Jhula Devi temple and the apple orchids. We then went to a local park with some swings, slides and basic rides. What was admirable about Ranikhet was that, from most places, we could see the same view of Himalayas! While Pinky was enjoying the rides, I got some time to speak to Karishma about Mukteshwar. The minute I informed her that I had already visited Mukteshwar temple alone as I did not want to risk their lives if something bad was about to happen, she was shocked and didn't speak to me for the rest of the day.

We reached the hotel in the evening and slept pretty early as we had a tiresome day as most of the time, we were on the move.

That night, I again got a dream. This time, I was standing in front of the main temple of Mukteshwar and I could see the sage sitting in the same position where I saw him this morning. The sage had asked me the same question that he had asked me in the morning.

"Do you want to know a Secret?"

This time, probably since it was a dream, I went and sat close to him and said,

"Yes, Maharaj" The word, 'Maharaj' which literally translates to King is usually used in India to address Sages.

"Then Son, you must first understand what you want to do? Tell me what is it that you want to do?"

"I want to earn money and be happy"

"Can you be more specific do you want to earn money and be happy or do you want to earn money to be happy?"

"Doesn't it mean the same thing?"

"There is a difference. Is money your goal or happiness? If your goal is happiness, money is one of the ways to achieve it; that too not for everyone."

Even in my dream, I had started getting irritated with the unsolicited speech and was about to get up and go when the sage held his hair and started tying a knot. What it did was to uncover his face and what I saw was a pure shock.

The sage had my exact face!

I again sat down and asked a different question.

"Who are you, Maharaj? Are you related to me? Are you the reason for this dream? Are you the link between me and the temple?"

The sage smiled and said "You will need to answer my questions if you really want to know who I am. And you will need to answer those truthfully from your heart"

I nodded.

"So, what is your goal? Is that happiness or money?"

"Of course Happiness!"

"Then how do you want to achieve it?"

"I want to earn money. I want to put up a good show in the office and try getting promotions. I will save from my salary to be happy in future...", when I was saying this, something struck me. *Saving for the future! Was I not convinced with what Mr. Mahapatra told about setting short targets and planning for the near future?*

As if the sage read my mind, he interrupted, "Do you think you can save enough money in the next few years?"

This question again took me away from Mr. Mahapatra's thoughts. "I want to wait and see for the next six months in the current organisation. If I am not satisfied, I will start my own business."

"Will you be happy then?"

"Of course, I will be! I will have more money to take care of all the necessities and luxuries of my family. I will be able to spend time with them, I will be able to do what I always wanted to do – learn a musical instrument, write a book, take my daughter for cycling daily, play with her more, spend more time with my wife, stay with my parents again and take care of them."

"Are you sure that these are the things that make you happy?"

"Yes, Absolutely!"

"Then who is stopping you from doing these things from today? Except for being able to spend more money on luxuries, I don't really see anything else in your list that cannot be done today. Why are you not doing those?"

I was surprised by this verbal attack. It took me a while to review and understand the question and it made absolute sense. But I didn't know the answer. But is that answer really important on why I wasn't doing the things that I liked? Instead, it is important that I start doing things that I love and the ones that bring happiness. But, what about money? How will I earn more money while being happy?

Again, I felt that the sage could read my mind.

"When you have a happy mind, you will find ways to earn money. You are very capable and your capabilities multiply when you are happy."

All this was sounding very logical to me. I replied, "Maharaj, thank you!"

"What is the secret that you were talking about?"

"This is the secret which you should know"

"Then how did I see this exact time in my dreams. This doesn't look logical at all. And how come you look exactly like me?"

"Everything that we see in this world is logical. The ones that sound illogical are the ones whose logic is not known. And coming to my face resembling yours'; it was always supposed to resemble yours. I am you; in your future!"

"Future! Do you mean that I am going to come over here and settle down?"

"Are you scared that you will become like me when you grow older?"

"No. No… I didn't mean to say that…" I was again interrupted by the sage's words.

"I am living in the Sanyasa phase of my life. But I thought you follow Mr. Mahapatra's advice of having the three stages – Learn, Live and Be Humble! I represent the Humble phase of your own life. Do you want to live your humble phase as a content man who achieved everything he wanted to? Once you are content, the place does not matter, you can live a calm, peaceful and humble life at your own house."

I was slowly realising that it is a dream even during the dream. I could easily correlate that all the lessons that I have been receiving in the past few weeks from different people were coming together to show me the correct direction.

-x-

When I woke up, I found my wife and daughter ready. My wife said, "Get up, Varun! We need to go to Mukteshwar. Even though you visited yesterday, I had promised God in my mind that I will offer prayers at Mukteshwar temple and it is not considered auspicious to break promises with God"

I was, myself thinking of visiting the temple again, to meet the Sage and see who he really was. I wanted to see his face and confirm that it is not me! Hence I got ready and we all started for Mukteshwar.

After close to ninety minutes, we were finally at Mukteshwar Temple. We had to carry my daughter over the stairs as she was exhausted after climbing twenty-odd stairs. By the time we reached the main temple, I was almost breathless. I sat down on the stairs and asked my wife and daughter to offer their prayers. After a few minutes, I got up and started searching for 'The Sage'. I could not find him anywhere. Then I went to the priest of the main temple and enquired about the Sage. But even he was clueless and had not seen any Sage with my face. It was anyways very difficult for him to recognise if he had seen someone with my face earlier.

I had not found the Sage, but I had learned the art of being calm. Maybe the time that I spent at the temple the previous day had enlightened me.

-x-

XIV

After spending some time at the temple, we descended from the temple hill and got into the cab. My daughter, for a change, was hungry and Mohammed took us to a decent restaurant in the town of Mukteshwar. My wife and I were mostly silent during the entire duration.

I was feeling different – I cannot really describe the feeling if it was satisfied, freed of unknown fear or confident of being able to overcome the unknowns. It was probably also due to the long-needed break from routine as recommended by Pallav, or the beauty of Muteshwar and Ranikhet, or due to the fact that I could spend some time to retrospect and understand how I should live my life, ably assisted by Mr. Mahapatra's advice and my dreams. It was not important on what made me feel this way, but what was important was the fact that I was feeling capable to handle the present situations that I have to face once I am back from vacation!

It took around an hour to reach Nainital, where we were to spend the rest of the day before starting for our return journey the next morning. Once in

Nainital, we checked into a hotel on the lakeside road and went out for a walk. Pinky requested Mohammed to join us too and he happily obliged. We went on boating in the Nainital Lake and once we were back to the shore, we sat on the benches nearby. Pinky had seen some kids play area on the shore somewhere while we were on the boat and was insisting on visiting the place. Mohammed volunteered to take her to the play area. We gave Mohammed some money, to pay for the tickets if there were any rides.

Once the duo left, Karishma and I started a walk on the lakeside, hand in hand, after more than three years. There was a cool breeze flowing, which made Karishma, hold my hand firmly while our shoulders were touching each other from time to time. At a point on the lakeshore, there were a few benches facing the lake. We sat on one of those, with smiles on our face and eyes stationed on each other, remembering our romantic walks from the past. After some time, I started staring into infinity beyond the lake and Karishma followed, not without asking, "Varun, so what's going on inside your mind?"

"Don't know! Karishma", I said after taking a long gap, thinking about my future.

"Hmm... I mean, how are you feeling? What did Mukteshwar reveal?"

"I am definitely feeling better but there was nothing unusual at Mukteshwar. It was normal and plain ordinary, except for the Sage who questioned me yesterday, appeared in my dream last night" and I narrated the Sage incident and the dream.

I concluded my narration with these words, "All I know is that the temple brought me inner calmness and allowed me to reconstruct my life. Throughout my life, I have been running behind important things like promotion or job. However, the time spent at the temple taught me to focus on minor things that bring happiness. I felt that I could build hundreds of such happy moments if I stop worrying about one huge goal. Also, the people whom I met in the last few weeks, Mr. Mahapatra, Pallav, Mohammed and others taught me something or the other. My dream helped me realise the importance of people in my life."

"Thank God Varun!" Karishma felt relieved after I explained to her the way I felt about life "Today, after so many days, I am feeling that I am talking to the old Varun whom I married."

These words made me realise for the first time that I was a changed man. All these years, deep into the office thoughts, late-night calls with clients, frequent ad-hoc business trips; all done with zeal to succeed and prove myself, had changed me entirely! I had just become a machine, running the rat race, day in and day out!

"Karishma! You never told me that I was behaving differently"

"You never say that to a person, deeply involved in thoughts! Else, you run the risk of losing that person forever"

I was feeling lucky to have such a wise wife. All I could do was hug her.

"That's ok, Varun! Enough of Public Display of Affection" she continued, "Varun, just be like this. You look awesome with a hearty smile"

I nodded. I knew how I want my life to be and also understood a few moments ago that even my wife agrees to my idea of being happy. But I still had to find answers to the 'how part' of it. *How will I be able to spend more time on myself and my family? Should I change my job? Should I confront my boss? What should I do?*

I am normally a very introvert person, especially in front of my family. That gives me a feeling that I am strong. However, today I felt that my wife is a stronger person than me and I wanted to discuss everything that was bothering me. Hence, I continued the conversation with the thoughts that were inside me, coming out without any filtering.

"Karishma, Should I change my job?"

"Should you?"

"You know how Adhoc life has become and there is absolutely no humanity in the way my organisation works"

"Varun, aren't organisations meant to be structured. Anything that is structured is, by default, un-human. Why is that even a criterion for you?"

"But my boss is not worthy enough to have me on his team. I do not perceive myself as superior but he is such a big …."

"Varun, I believe in your decision and will support you wholeheartedly. But is there a guarantee that you have a better work culture in the new job?" After a pause, she continued, "Have you thought about changing your project? In a way, change your boss, not the organisation!"

"Leave the boss! That is actually a cool idea! Let me think over it. I can opt for a transfer to a different division within my organisation and get rid of Omkaar and Arnab. Wow! Why did I not think of this? But I have to do this carefully. It is a very political situation…." I kept on thinking aloud for the next 1-2 minutes while Karishma patiently listened to me and finally interrupted.

"You don't have to solve this problem today! Is your boss the only problem? Give it some time and think over it.", Karishma said with a grin.

I smiled back but still wanted to flush out everything that came in my mind, so I continued, "Karishma, this is important. Let me figure this out. First thing when I join the office, I will try to change my division. Whether or not I succeed, I will not let my job dictate my behaviour. Although, I am not happy with my current role, should I really give it a lot of importance? My job is just to earn me money to take care of the family. Why should I be emotionally connected to it?"

Karishma was patiently listening while I continued, "From now on, my job is just a necessity in my life."

"I love you Varun!" was the only response from Karishma.

I looked towards Karishma with a grateful smile and in the background; my eyes could see Pinky jumping happily with one hand in Mohammed's and the other hand holding three heart-shaped helium balloons. Pinky was obviously happy with this trip and whenever she is happy, it makes my day!

That night, I slept and I slept really well! The next morning, we started back to Delhi. After almost a week, I enabled the internet on my mobile and started checking my personal messages. Of all the messages, the one that gave me satisfaction was that of Pallav. Pallav had responded to my last email! It read,

"Dear Varun,

Apologies, I could not respond to your email earlier. I am currently on a vacation trip to India. I am currently in Jaipur, my hometown.

Congratulations on finding your dream temple! Please visit it if you can! Less than one percent of people who can remember their dreams are able to find the place in reality. Let me know what you found at the temple. I am sure, once you visit the temple, your attachment to the dream would be reduced and you will be back to your regular self. It will also give you the much-needed break that you deserve!

Warm Regards,

Pallav"

Pallav had shared his contact # with me in the email. I immediately called him up.

"Hello! This is Pallav speaking"

"Hi Pallav, this is Varun! Sravan's friend. How are you doing?"

"Hey, Varun! It is nice to hear from you. I am doing good. How are you doing?"

"I am good too. Are you still in Jaipur? I am near Delhi right now. Getting back from Mukteshwar"

"Hey, that's cool. Why don't you drop into Jaipur for a few days? It is just a four-hour drive from Delhi"

"That sounds good... but I have to join the office on Monday."

"Monday is still two days away! Come by, we can discuss your Mukteshwar observations. I am keen on knowing that"

I was tempted to say yes but said, "Pallav, it might be difficult. I have my flight booked for tonight. However, let me call you once I am in Hyderabad. We will discuss everything as even I want to bring it to proper closure."

"As you wish, Varun"

We greeted each other and dropped the call.

Once in Delhi, we had a couple of hours left before the flight. We wanted to purchase something for my parents. We went to Connaught Place – Palika Bazaar, an underground street shopping famous for clothes, shoes, electronics, gifts, and toys. When we went inside, Pinky wanted to buy a shirt for Mohammed. She had apparently seen Mohammed wearing a torn shirt and was feeling bad. We bought two shirts and a pair of sandals for Mohammed. We also bought a sweater for my mom and a cap for my dad before leaving for the airport.

At the airport, Mohammed was emotional when we gave him a farewell gift. He had actually purchased a toy elephant for Pinky. We were moved by his gesture. We promised to meet him every time we visited Delhi.

Inside the airport, once we checked in, Karishma asked me an important question, "So, what do we tell mom? Do we tell her that we visited Mukteshwar or not?"

"We will tell her the truth! I know it would be scary but I think it is the best thing to do and put an end to this episode."

The return flight was again on time and we landed in Hyderabad on time. By the time we reached home, it was well past dinner time but my parents were waiting for us to have dinner together.

We got freshened up and sat for dinner. At the dinner table, my parents asked about the trip and we told about everything – the Ranikhet trip, Kausani trip, uncle Mahendra's hospitality, etc. except Mukteshwar.

As we were about to finish dinner, I said to my mom, "Mom! We went to Mukteshwar!"

I could immediately see her eyes deepen, eyebrows raise and lines appear on her forehead.

"I didn't find anything unusual there. It was exactly the temple that I saw in my dream. We offered our prayers and came back."

She was scared and turned towards Karishma and said, "I told you and you promised me that you will not go to Mukteshwar! Why do you do such dangerous things? Don't you love me?"

"Mom! We are back and we are fine. Nothing happened", I tried to console her.

"What if something would have happened?"

"Sorry, mom! I had to do that. I didn't have an option. Now I have a fresh mind"

Mom didn't speak anything after that. She went to the temple area within our house and thanked all the deities for my safe return and went to her bedroom saying, "Never do such things!!"

-x-

The next morning, I called up Pallav and narrated him the entire Mukteshwar episode, the dream that I had and how the dream summarised the thoughts!

"Pallav, I never thought that dreams could be so soothingly warm to guide me in my life"

"Varun! That is the beauty of our minds. It picks up incredible amounts of information that we cannot absorb or assimilate in our senses, and it can even analyse this information based on ideas we aren't even aware of unconsciously. In your case, it even simplified and expressed the summary in a beautiful way, all this, while you were sleeping! Incredible!"

"But, there are still a few open questions. How did I get this dream in the first place? Why was the temple looking so familiar to me?"

"Varun, you might have seen the temple somewhere, probably on television. Scientifically, I cannot think of any other possibility."

"Possible. But it doesn't matter to me now. My trip did only favour to me by bringing my thinking back on track!"

-x-

Monday morning, I reached the office before 9 am. As usual, the office was deserted with I being the only soul at that time. After plugging in my laptop at my cubicle, I walked out of my office zone and went to the fifth floor to meet my friend Madan, who was another punctual soul in the office like me. Madan and I had worked together five years ago and had developed a great brotherly bond over the years. Although we work in the same organisation, we could not meet often due to our own commitments. Whenever we would meet, it would be at the pantry or the office canteen for a casual chat. Madan was leading another group within my organisation and I had spoken to him, the day before, on the possibility of joining his project.

I went to his floor and knocked on the glass door, as I did not have access to his office zone. He saw me from inside and came out to let me in.

I went to his cubicle, which was half closed but was not shared by anyone else. Madan had intentionally rejected a closed cubicle as he wanted to be seated with his team.

The conversation started on a direct note with Madan saying, "Varun, I believe, you want to discuss your project change."

I nodded and said, "Madan, as I told you yesterday over the phone, I am not feeling comfortable working with Arnab and Omkaar. Our frequencies do not match."

"I know Arnab. He is a spineless creature! I was actually surprised how you survived so long?" Madan was aware of my character and knew exactly the kind of problems I might have faced with Arnab. He continued, "I suggest, you wait for a few weeks. We just won a new project deal. It should materialise in the next two-three weeks. We can definitely take you in that project. I will be leading that project."

"Thank You, Madan. That will be awesome!"

Madan smiled, "Varun, you don't have to thank me. You are a treat to work with! Accha… while waiting for this project to materialise, why don't you take a few weeks off and go out somewhere? That way, you don't have to see Arnab's face" said Madan with a cunning smile.

"That's difficult actually! I am joining today after a few weeks off."

"Wow! Did you go out somewhere?"

"Yes. We went to Ranikhet, my first vacation in the last two years." While I said Ranikhet, I could see some excitement on Madan's face.

"Wow! That is one awesome place. Did you also go to Mukteshwar?"

"Yes. How do you know Mukteshwar?"

"Come on. I got married at Mukteshwar. Don't you remember that? My wife is from Kumaon."

"Oh really! How did I forget that!"

"That's because you did not attend my wedding." Madan was teasing me.

"Madan, I was in the US when you got married." While I said this, my mind was already trying to decipher if Madan's Mukteshwar connect was something that caused me, my dream?

"Yeah! I know. You saw my marriage pictures on Picasa and even commented on those. Now you forgot where I got married."

I suddenly remembered that. "Yes…Yes… Thank you!!"

Madan was puzzled about what I was saying. I could read that by looking at his face. I reduced the intensity of animation in my expressions and said, "Do you have the link now? Can I see the pictures?"

"Let me check." Madan opened his email account and started searching. "Here they are!"

As I went closer to the screen to see the pictures, I only realised two things. One was the fact that the pictures were exactly like the temple that I saw in my dream. Secondly, Madan had to wear a crown on his head as per the traditions of the wedding.

I was very relaxed. I had found the source of the visuals of my dream! How big a fool I was! I had made a big issue of something so small!

"What happened Varun?" asked a still baffled Madan.

"Nothing Madan! I had a sense of Déjà vu in the Mukteshwar temple that was making me uncomfortable. Now I understand why I felt so."

"Ok...For a few seconds, I could not understand why you are suddenly interested in my wedding pictures."

The meeting ended after a few minutes of casual chat about our families. I was extremely satisfied that day, probably; this discovery of the source of the dream would be added to the collection of my happy moments!

Once I came out of the zone, I called up Karishma and then Pallav. I told them about the source of the dream and we had a good laugh.

I went back to my cubicle, checked my emails without really expecting anything. Things were as usual in the office too. *Nothing changed, with or without my presence in the office.* I was far more relaxed in my approach and closed my work sharp at 6 pm. After reaching home, I could spend some time with family and also read a bedtime story to Pinky.

This is how our lives are! Life is neither simple nor complicated. It is just a journey. The better we know our companions and the route, the simpler it appears. The farther we think about the journey and spend extra effort in planning the intricate turns and exits, the complicated it becomes! At the same time, if we don't know the route even for the next few miles, we will remain clueless throughout the journey!

Life is very short and it will always find ways to keep us busy. Hence, it is extremely important for us to have a 'checkpoint' on our own lives from time to time, to retrospect if we are in sync with our dreams, goals, and desires. This retrospection can help us plan or re-plan our near future.

While I was happy with the way I had started approaching my life, I still wanted to hit the 'Positive Black Swan' and wanted to work towards it. However, I wanted to do that as a hobby and not join the rat race again. I will share that episode of my life with all of you, some other time, after I hit the Positive Black Swan. Until then, happy life!

-x-

Printed in Poland
by Amazon Fulfillment
Poland Sp. z o.o., Wrocław

54997717R00094